THE
PUNISHING
JOURNEY
OF
ARTHUR
DELANEY

THE
PUNISHING
JOURNEY
OF
ARTHUR
DELANEY

a novel

BOB KROLL

Published by ECW Press
665 Gerrard Street East
Toronto, Ontario, Canada M4M 1Y2
416-694-3348 / info@ecwpress.com

Cover design: Sophie Paas-Lang

LIBRARY AND ARCHIVES CANADA CATALOGUING
IN PUBLICATION

Title: The punishing journey of Arthur Delaney : a
novel / Bob Kroll.

Names: Kroll, Bob, 1947- author.

Identifiers: Canadiana (print) 20210398655 |
Canadiana (ebook) 20210398671

ISBN 978-1-77041-633-8 (softcover)
ISBN 978-1-77305-937-2 (ePub)
ISBN 978-1-77305-938-9 (PDF)
ISBN 978-1-77305-939-6 (Kindle)

Classification: LCC PS8621.R644 P86 2022 |
DDC C813/.6—dc23

This book is funded in part by the Government of Canada. *Ce livre est financé en partie par le gouvernement du Canada.*
We acknowledge the support of the Canada Council for the Arts. *Nous remercions le Conseil des arts du Canada de son
soutien.* We acknowledge the support of the Ontario Arts Council (OAC), an agency of the Government of Ontario,
which last year funded 1,965 individual artists and 1,152 organizations in 197 communities across Ontario for a total of
$51.9 million. We also acknowledge the support of the Government of Ontario through the Ontario Book Publishing
Tax Credit, and through Ontario Creates.

PRINTED AND BOUND IN CANADA   PRINTING: MARQUIS   5   4   3   2   1

In memory of
Brian McRory and Andrew Stiles

CHAPTER 1

An old man in bib overalls drove a rumbling farm wagon along a Pennsylvania country road. He ducked low branches, which printed the road in sun dapples and long, sleepy shadows. He talked to his horse as a way of talking to himself.

Up ahead, where the road swung close to the river, he saw a stranger hailing to hitch a ride. He saw the dew prints where the stranger had walked up from the river and across the meadow. He saw trails of white smoke by the river from a campfire that had been doused. He saw the stranger's trousers wet to the knees and his duffle bag in his hand and his bedroll carried bandolier-style across his chest. When the stranger got close, the driver saw the cuts and bruises on the stranger's rough-hewn face, the stranger's split knuckles, the wince and shoulder hitch and careful way the stranger held his rib cage when he pulled himself onto the wagon.

"Where you going?" the old man asked, settling low in the seat, with his knees up around his ears. He flicked the reins to remind the horse that he was driving. His voice was high-pitched like a wheel squeak.

"Just anywhere, so long as it's northeast," the stranger replied. He tried on a smile that didn't quite fit. His clothes didn't quite fit either, like they had shrunk after he had pulled them on. His hat fit, however, a blue Union Army kepi.

"You don't have far to get *there*," the driver said, and sneaked a canny look the stranger's way. "Just anywhere seems like it's a distance. Give it time, and just anywhere will be right around the bend. Settle there and soon enough you'll be calling it home." He chuckled and flicked the reins.

"I won't be settling," the stranger said.

The driver smiled. "You never know about the twists and turns and the changing light. A blast of snow most always has us wintering out."

The stranger undid his bedroll and set it in back. He inched his eyes the driver's way, then rested them on the horse's rump.

The dusty road kept pace with the river, which slowed into deep pools all shadowy under a heavy canopy of sycamore and black willow. Now and again the low sun breached the treeline and flashed on the water. A rabbit darted off the road ahead. A trout jumped and splashed not far from where a farmer was loading half a dozen cows onto a barge for ferrying to a small island. One cow was reluctant to board, and the farmer fanned it with his hat.

The driver offered the stranger a chew and they chewed and spit. The stranger launched the juice over his left shoulder and with the breeze. The driver rolled the plug from cheek to cheek and spit at a tuft of hair on the horse's rump, like it was a target.

A red-shouldered hawk flew above the river. As the stranger watched it circling, the driver studied the shiner and bruises on the right side of the stranger's face. He knew where they had come from, a warehouse near the woollen mill at Gurdy Run.

The stranger caught him looking.

"I saw you the other night," the driver confessed. "Was it worth it?"

The stranger shrugged as though it was nothing. "I knew I could last three rounds."

The driver shook his head. "Against a man with high leather boots and built with muscle on top of muscle, there's easier ways to earn five dollars."

"Not these days," the stranger said, and looked past the driver and beyond the river to a white farmhouse neatly tucked into rolling hills.

"Most soldiers mustered out and come home when the war was done in 'sixty-five," the driver said. "Whatever work there is they're at it. What took you so long?"

The stranger continued looking at the farmhouse. "A Confederate prison in North Carolina. It took nearly two years to heal up."

"How long you in there?"

"Captured at Sessionville," the stranger said.

"Three years in prison is nothing to wink at," the driver said. "Damn war ruined a lot of everything. Who knew it would last so long?"

The road dipped and ran level with the river for a ways. The driver had to negotiate logs and tree limbs flung up on the road by a run of high water. Cinnamon fern grew in a flood plain meadow between the road and the river.

"How far north you going?" the driver pressed.

"A long ways," the stranger said, still looking at the farmhouse and the hills. "Nova Scotia."

"I don't know it," the driver said.

"East of Maine."

"East of Maine is just water. I know that much."

"And Nova Scotia is in the middle of it."

The driver searched the road ahead as though searching for something he had misplaced or lost. He turned back to the stranger. "There's work in a tannery the next town over. Dirty work, but sometimes you take what you can get."

The stranger nodded.

"I got a piece not far from the mill. It's not much. There's a woman there too, and her mother, and a girl child. They live in a shack on my land. They ain't mine. They belong to a no-account named Billy Wood. He works up through Scranton area. Robbing banks, for all I know. He goes away, comes back. Months usually. This time it's been over a year. He used her the same way that boxer used you. She's got no one else. You can bunk in the barn. Take meals in the house. Work your keep or pay rent from wages if it works out punching hides at the tannery. Don't matter to me."

Again the stranger nodded. His smile fit his face a little easier.

"My name's Murdock Murray." The driver offered his hand.

The stranger shook it. "Arthur Delaney."

Murray leaned and pulled a jug from behind the seat and reached it to Delaney as a way of capping off the introductions and sealing a deal. "Never too early, that's what I always say."

Delaney shook it off. "Thanks, but I couldn't hold it down."

Murray took a long pull, wiped his mouth, and returned the jug behind the seat.

"I'm guessing that boxer made a mess of your insides," he said.

"Seems so."

They rode in silence for a while. Delaney tried closing his eyes, but the pain shooting through his skull and the see-saw of the wagon turned his stomach. He had taken so many jabs and several solid rights to the head that sunlight off the water was a blister on his brain. His inability to heave a deep breath didn't help his comfort either. Yeah, he got knuckled pretty good, knocked silly but not out. No rules. Just bare-knuckles boxing. Elbows and knees permitted. He was still standing after three rounds with that boxer who was nothing but grit and gristle, a powerful man who danced circles and then spirals around that warehouse floor. Dizzying amidst a flurry of left and rights that snapped back Delaney's head and pummelled his belly. Coughing up his guts. Doubled over and on his knees as pails of beer passed among the crowd, swilling and letting it leak down their chins and chests, men and women shoulder-to-shoulder, their tortured faces screwed into awkward smiles stirred with the savage love of violence and blood. A rage of sweat. Fingers clenching and unclenching to see one man beat the other to a pulp. Knocked down but not knocked out, not for the count, not for five dollars that he later stashed in a drawstring pouch tucked inside his bedroll.

"You look like hell," Murray said.

"Feel it too."

"Climb in back and stretch out. It'll do you good."

"I can't lie flat. My head pounds harder if I do. I slept upright against a tree last night. Tied myself to it."

"Then rest against a feed bag."

Delaney climbed in back and did as suggested. Once settled he let himself go dozy with the rhythmic clop of the horse and rattle of the wagon. Not so much daydreaming, but lost to ragged thoughts that were illuminated behind the flashes of pain. Listening to Murray talking to the horse but not hearing what he said. Looking through the passing trees and beyond the river where he saw the long plume of grey smoke before, he heard the train blow for a crossing.

The wagon rumbled on as Delaney fingered an itch on his thigh, a tickle beneath his skin. He swallowed hard and winced at the rush of pain in his ribs and chest, pain like heartache. He looked back along the road the wagon had travelled. Along the road he had travelled. Looking back and feeling afraid that all he had left behind would someday disappear. He struggled with sleep. After a while it crept over him.

✦

He opened his eyes and realized the wagon had stopped in a farmyard set back from the road by a long wagon-way. There was a kitchen garden on one side and scabby apple trees on the other. Beyond the garden was a small stand of sugar maple with taps still in the trees and collecting buckets scattered on the ground. A spruce windbreak flanked a caved woodshed and chicken coop. The barn wasn't much, and the farmhouse needed paint.

From inside the barn, a cow bellowed and a couple of sheep bleated. Chickens ranged in the farmyard, and on the south side of the house, a draft horse nervously walked the fence line of a paddock.

Delaney painfully rolled to his feet and climbed from the wagon. He called for Murdock Murray, who hollered back from inside the barn. Delaney followed the voice to find the farmer squatting under the cow and squirting milk into a pail.

"She knows nothing about farm work," Murray complained without lifting his eyes, punctuating his words by ringing the milk off the side of the pail. "What she does know don't come often enough to set a clock." He stopped milking and sat for a moment staring at his hands on the teats and the frothy milk in the pail. "I can't manage it alone. It takes more than one."

Delaney shifted uneasily. "You got something you want me to do?"

Murray nodded and splashed milk into the pail. "Stable the mare. Wipe her down. The draft in the paddock keeps her company."

Delaney started for the door, then looked back to see Murray's face drawn and distant, the milk splashing off the rim of the pail and onto the barn floor.

Delaney had the mare unhitched and stabled and was fetching the draft when he saw her coming from the house, child in her arms, long brown hair blowing up with the easy wind off the field. She gave him her hand and introduced herself as Maggie Francis.

His own name was wobbly off his flattened tongue. He fixed on her thin face, studied it. Her cheeks and forehead were pale to her dark hair and eyes. Her lips were parted as though she meant to say more, but didn't.

He watched her all the way to the barn and all the way back to the house, carrying the child and pail of milk, grey smock over a frayed brown dress that trailed in the dust. Nothing pretty, just plain, like a crocheted shawl.

Later Delaney painfully split stove wood and watched her bucket water from the well. She lugged the heavy bucket and slopped water on her dress and over her bare feet.

During supper his eyes kept finding her wherever they looked. Serving stew from a catch pot on the back of the cast iron stove; Murray first, then Delaney, then her mother, who slowly rocked beside the wood box for warmth. The mother's face cleaved deep with wrinkles like the crenels in brown paper. His eyes again drifted the young woman's way and watched her feed her one-year-old daughter, who had copper-coloured hair. Her name was Abby. He smiled to remember Annie, his youngest, when she was a baby, with her teeth clenched and mouth sealed against his effort to feed her.

Maggie Francis served herself and sat beside Delaney. She toyed with her food as though eating was the furthest thing from her mind and the least of her needs.

"We don't say grace," Murray announced and tucked into his stew, slurping without ceremony.

Maggie offered Delaney bread and he tore off a hunk. "Murdock says you were soldiering."

He picked up on the slight drawl in her voice, and that southern sound twigged a trouble deep inside. He nodded.

"The Rebels made you a prisoner," she continued.

Again he nodded, and as he dipped his bread, his eyes emptied to a memory of that Confederate prison.

"I heard them Rebs treated our boys poorly," Murray said.

Delaney nodded. He saw himself opening the hatch to the cellar in an abandoned cotton warehouse. The Johnny Reb corporal standing over him and gagging on the rising stink. Delaney removed his neckerchief and held it over a camphor pot to catch the flames. He tied the neckerchief over his nose and mouth. He doused his blue kepi in the fumes and pulled it low on his head. He waited as the corporal struck a lantern and passed it to him. He descended the ladder into the darkness of a large vault with a mud floor. In the widening cone of light, he saw the sick and starved faces of Union soldiers. Some ducked from the light, others stared at him. Beyond them there were more faces and beyond them more and more.

"Maine is a long way off," said Murdock Murray. "And you still got a ways left to where you're going."

"I do," Delaney said. "Four or five hundred miles."

Murray slurped a spoonful of stew.

From her rocker beside the wood box, the old woman chirped, "That's not in America."

Murray smiled at Delaney. "A place not in America can't be just anywhere. And if it's not just anywhere then it must be somewhere, and if it's somewhere then it might as well be here. You should use my name if you go looking for work."

He and Murray now stacked the stove wood Delaney had split earlier beneath a lean-to with open sides. It could go a few months with the wind blowing through and drying it. Murray talked the entire time. His squeaky voice muffled when he told about his wife dying from the sweating sickness and his four-year-old son dying too. Thirty-something years and he still pained over it. He buried them both in a plot on the knoll behind the house. The two of them in the same grave because it seemed fitting they should be together.

He asked if Delaney had family. Delaney nodded and grabbed an armload of wood from the pile beside the chopping block and carried it to the lean-to for stacking.

"I never met a man more stingy with words," Murray said, as they walked to the woodshed attached to the kitchen.

Delaney stacked the newly split wood and loaded up on dry for the cookstove. Murray carried kindling. The kitchen door slapped behind them.

Maggie was cleaning dishes. Delaney emptied his load in the bin behind the cookstove and started out for another. She turned quickly, catching him at the door.

"You don't talk much," she said, and turned back to washing, sneaking her eyes to his reflection in the dark window above the sink.

He looked at Murray, who cocked his head in a told-you-so gesture.

Delaney faced her. He met her eyes in the window, seeing her sad face disguised by a smile, a young woman burdened with a child and an aging mother. Her hardened jaw, her laugh lines channelled deep. He saw something else in the young woman's face, something he saw in himself whenever he looked into the cracked mirror that he carried in his duffle — eyes that had lost their sparkle.

"Talk stirs up things in my head," he said. "Most are better left not talked about."

She nodded as though she appreciated his safeguard. "Murdock could use a good hand," she said, and lowered her eyes and dunked her hands for another plate.

"I need work to keep going on," he said, and left the kitchen for the woodshed.

⚜

Later that night Delaney carried a lantern to the barn and hung it on a wooden pin stuck into one of the posts. He sat cross-legged on the leather harness and blankets he had piled for a bunk. He looked over his accommodation. To his carpenter's eye he saw it right away. He got up and went around to look at the horse stalls beside his. The mare and the draft fit comfortably, side by side, and lengthwise. He looked at his stall. He did not need a string to see the horses would not fit the length of it.

The empty hay crib hung loosely from the back wall. He removed it. About chest high he saw finger holds carefully cut and filed into two tight-fitting boards. It took little effort to remove a panel that was less than a foot wide. Behind it he found a cramped space two feet deep and the width of the horse stall. There was a dirty white scarf on the floor of it.

He replaced the panel and hay crib and returned to sitting cross-legged on the harness and blankets.

"A runaway's hidey-hole is not my business," he said to himself.

From his bedroll he withdrew a carving knife and a chunk of maple. He started shaping the chunk into the rough figure of a doll. After a while, he set the knife and wood aside and sat wakeful to the sound of the night circling up from the river and closing him off from the world. He heard a nighthawk screeching across a field beside the barn, and a dog barking from somewhere along the road. He heard the lonely sound of his own breathing and of his mind scratching at a scab of regret, the way it had scratched his mind raw the night before he was to sail from Halifax to Boston, to join the 28th Massachusetts Volunteers.

He had gone to Miss Golding's Children's Refuge and Aid Home for one chance to see his children before he left for Boston. The lights were out in the front rooms of the downstairs. He had slipped along the cinder driveway to the horse stable and carriage house. He crouched in the shadows against a stable wall and pressed his face against the rough-sawn boards, angling a view through the big windows of the scullery. He saw a woman pointing to where she wanted two boys to stow two huge copper pots. And then Miss Golding entered and inspected the scullery for tidiness. Seeing her had made his back hairs tingle. Then the light went out in the scullery, and Delaney had lifted his eyes to the dormitory upstairs. At such a sharp angle, he saw nothing on the curtained windows, not even shadows.

He got up from the harness and blanket bunk and opened the barn door and looked at the starlight silvering the field of timothy and clover: a hayfield that needed mowing and drying and storing in the barn loft where he heard a cat hunting mice. He saw a farm going to seed, and wondered about Murray being too old to keep up.

Murdock could use a hand, she had said, as though *he* were the hand Murdock needed.

He looked beyond the field to the road for going home. A similar road he had marched down to go to war, a coward's road for all he had left behind. A long road made longer by the prison hell he had suffered.

"The war'll be over before you know it," the abolitionist preacher had promised. He stood in the pulpit of a church in

Halifax, speaking to a hundred or so men and women, their upturned faces sweat-polished from hymn-singing on a hot summer night. They eagerly listened to the preacher's every word. "A month, six at the most," he had said. "A scant sacrifice for the glory of God and the freedom of the slaves."

Delaney had taken those words as gospel. He made his mark on the enlistment form the way his wife had taught him how, with a flourish on the final letter — Y.

A year into the war, and then his capture at Sessionville. Be over before you know it, the abolitionist preacher had promised. That was no more than a bond broken a thousand times and buried with the bodies he had dragged from the dark cellar of that prison. The "bone-picker," the guards had called him. An undertaker dressed in dead man's clothes. A punishment bereft of rescue.

He closed the barn door and returned to sitting cross-legged on his bunk. Hesitant to blow out the light. Afraid the dead would talk to him, call him by name. Delaney. Arthur Delaney.

CHAPTER 2

S pencer led Sheriff Greene into the kitchen where a young woman and a girl sat at a long pine table set with bowls of porridge and a plate of muffins spread with butter and blueberry jam. The younger one had satisfied her hunger. The young woman had poked at her food. Sheriff Greene guessed her age at fifteen, maybe older, all elbows and knees, with long brown hair that hung just anyway around a long face made longer by a leaden look of sadness. She wore a blue jumper that had a large reddish-brown stain on the front and on the sides. Mud caked on the hem.

He guessed the little one at twelve. She now sat shying behind the bigger girl. She too wore a blue jumper with mud caked on the hem. Her jumper had a big rip up one side and a shoulder strap torn off. She had brown hair cut short in the shape of a bowl, and a curious gaze that sneaked around the kitchen, settling on Spencer's wife standing at the stove, and then on Spencer and Sheriff Greene in the doorway.

"Who do we have here?" Sheriff Greene asked, and his husky voice snapped the younger girl's eyes forward and frightened her to curl up tight against the older girl. The size of him didn't help set either one of them at ease.

Spencer's wife stepped from the stove to halt his advance into the kitchen. She angled herself between the men in the doorway and the girls at the table. She had eyes like stove lids and the beefy arms of a farm wife.

"The little one said her name is Annie Delaney," Spencer's wife whispered so the children wouldn't hear. "She talks, but not much. The big one, Robina, is her sister. She hasn't said a word. She's like a statue when I talk to her. I could tell a man in the house frightened them."

"She shooed me out," Spencer griped.

His wife looked at Sheriff Greene.

Sheriff Greene nodded, looked the girls over good, then backed from the house into the farmyard. Spencer and his wife followed him out.

"Did the little one say where they're from?" Sheriff Greene asked.

Spencer's wife shrugged. "The Island is all she said."

"Moose Island?"

"Must be. They were coming from up river."

"That's a two-day walk," Sheriff Greene said.

"I saw them from the field," Spencer piped. He was older than his wife, bald and stooped. "They were walking the side of the road. Not so much walking as creeping, you know, like they were scared. I hollered to the wife who was hanging clothes."

Spencer's wife confirmed. "I watched them for a while, then I called. They walked up. The little one did, anyway. The big one just followed, like she was on a leash. I dipped them a drink from the well, and said I had breakfast if they wanted. I never knew a child that wasn't hungry. It took a while to get them inside. Coaxing. A warm kitchen, and them out here with no jacket or scarf."

"Moose Island," the Sheriff mused. "Living with Dooley Smith, you suppose?"

"They must have been working there," Spencer's wife said. "The little one didn't say where, but she said they did farm chores and keeping house."

"He'd need the help with his wife dying," Spencer added.

Sheriff Greene pulled a pipe from his back pocket and filled it from a brown leather pouch. He addressed Spencer's wife. "I'd like to know about that stain on the big one's dress. Do you think you could ask about it?"

"You know what it looks like to me?" Spencer said.

"Yeah I know," Sheriff Greene replied. He turned to Spencer's wife. "Just keep pressing about how they come to Moose Island and what they were doing there. And ask about their parents."

Spencer's wife went back inside. She was in there a long time. When she came out, Spencer was watering Sheriff Greene's horse, and Sheriff Greene was standing on the road looking in the direction the girls had come.

"Annie wouldn't say much," Spencer's wife said. "I think the big one shushed her after seeing you. When I asked about their father and mother, the big one went real tense and Annie started crying."

❧

Sheriff Greene rode out at sunrise, the fallen leaves crisp with frost. He reached Daniel Harley's place late that afternoon. Harley, a tall, thin man with a rubbery face and small, fidgety hands, was in the barn replacing cribbed boards on a horse stall. Sheriff Greene held the new boards in place while Harley hammered.

Harley said he hadn't seen Dooley Smith in six months, maybe eight, not since Muriel had died. He knew about the girls. After his wife had taken sick, Smith hired them from some people in Nova Scotia who had bonded them from an orphanage. They were good workers, from what Jenny Pierce had said. Harley had a raft tied up at a landing across the river from Moose Island. He had ferried Jenny over half a dozen times to look after Muriel. He offered to ferry Sheriff Greene come morning. He also offered the Sheriff supper and a bed in a back shed where he bunked hired hands during the harvest.

Sheriff Greene accepted the ferry ride and the bunkhouse. He declined supper. He wanted to talk with Jenny Pierce and thought he would take supper there.

The Pierce place was a two-by-twice cabin set down off the road in a hollow. It was so small, a shadow would have had difficulty finding a wall to lean against. Three for supper made for tight quarters.

Jenny, a wiry little thing with a long face, popping eyes, and quick hands, scoured potatoes and seasoned a shank of beef. Billy Pierce and Sheriff Greene split stove wood in the woodshed. Pierce was a stumpy, powerfully built man who worked the woods for the Cumming's operation up river.

"I got nothing good to say about Dooley Smith," Billy Pierce volunteered when he learned why Sheriff Greene had come. For punctuation, he exploded his axe through a stick of maple. "He was mean as a boy and got meaner with age. It's a good thing he lives on that island or we would have tangled a lot more times than we did. Muriel had her hands full, let me tell you. His kids too, they run off as soon as they come of age. But you ask Jenny. She knows how he treated his own. I'm sure he treated those girls he got the same way."

Pierce split two more sticks of maple and one of yellow birch, then slammed the axe into the chopping block. His face screwed tight as he lifted his eyes to Sheriff Greene. "He blamed his wife because she got sick. He beat her black and blue."

After supper, Pierce returned to the woodshed to sharpen his axe and saws, and Sheriff Greene helped Jenny with the dishes. The house might have been small but it was homey, scrubbed wooden floors and frilly curtains.

"I can't blame those girls for running away," Jenny said, and squeaked a thumb up the inside of a coffee mug. "He worked them hard, I can tell you that."

Sheriff Greene picked a chipped plate from the drain board and dried it carefully, quiet, letting her talk as she wanted, letting her say what he sensed was eating at her confidence. She pumped clean rinse water into a basin and started on the pots, stopped, looked out the window above the sink, looked deep into the darkness outside.

"Muriel knew what was going on," Jenny said, as much to herself as to Sheriff Greene. "And she knew that I knew."

Jenny reached for a pot to scrub. Stopped. She sank into her shoulders and her eyes filled. "There was nothing I could do. I tried. I told him what I thought and he run me off the island. Threatened me if I came back. I never told Billy. And I never went back, not even after Muriel died."

Jenny rinsed the pot and set it on the drain board. She turned to face Sheriff Greene. "But it ain't runaway girls that brought you here."

CHAPTER 3

❧

Delaney hired on at the tannery, using Murdock Murray's name to land the job. Twelve hours, six days a week. He and two other fellows, Wendell Colley and Joseph Dearborn, both of them freed slaves, carted fresh hides from the slaughterhouse, which was a half-mile from the tannery. They salted the hides, rolled them tight, and packed them away to cure. Cured hides they carried to the beamhouse, where Delaney, Colley, and Dearborn limed them and scudded them of residual flesh and hair.

Sometimes they collected bones and horns from the slaughterhouse and brought them to a side building at the tannery for boiling into glue. They scraped gristle from bones, then barrowed them over a rickety catwalk and dumped them into a steamy iron vat, rendering them to a thick liquid, which was set out in the sun and dried hard.

Colley and Dearborn kept to themselves, working quietly, saying little to Delaney. A white man working alongside two former slaves. Sharing the load. Doing no less than they did.

After three weeks of keeping their distance, Dearborn offered Delaney some of his meat and vegetable pastry, which he brought for lunch almost every day. Delaney shared a hunk of beef jerky. The following day, Delaney brought a dented gunpowder tin filled with stewed beans and turnip. It was as though the food sharing had chinked mortar from the wall that separated them. They started talking, mostly during the wagon rides to and from the slaughterhouse.

Colley did the driving. Delaney and Dearborn rode in back on a stack of boards. The boards they used for separating each tier of hides. Colley said he knew all about Canada and about the Underground Railroad that helped escaped slaves travel north to freedom. He had a sister who chanced a freedom run. She made it to Buffalo, Colley said, and then across a big lake to Canada. She had sent word to him saying so.

Colley had been a field slave. To hear him tell it, he was too black to be a house slave. Besides, he was strong enough for the back-breaking labour on a Virginia tobacco plantation.

"I was sold down river after my sister's escape," he said. "Worked a Mississippi plantation. Ditching and hoeing and picking cotton. Field hollering to soften the work."

Dearborn told about working as hard and as long as a freeman as he did as a slave. The difference being free meant the fruit of his labour was all his, to do with as he wanted. He said the house he lived in was his too. So was the field he ploughed and the draft he ploughed it with.

Then Colley grumbled something about good jobs going to white folk and then started singing:

Who are those children all dressed in red?
God's gonna trouble the water.
Must be the ones that Moses led.
God's gonna trouble the water.

Dearborn leaned forward and asked Delaney how come he took up fighting in a war that wasn't his.

Delaney was slow to answer. He stared at the passing trees, one hand kneading the other.

Dearborn gave him time. Listening to Colley singing. Joining Colley on the chorus.

Finally Delaney said, his voice muffled in Colley's singing and in the horse clop and rattling wheels, "My wife died, and I feared raising my three children on my own. I gave them up to a woman named Miss Golding. The abolitionist talk made for an easy excuse for me to leave and join up."

He looked at the tattered kepi in his hands. His fingers picked at its frayed stitches. His eyes filled remembering Miss Golding's office, where she sat behind a walnut desk in a pool of light cast from a brass oil lamp with a pink-coloured shade of etched glass.

He stood at the door to her office, taken by the polished furnishings and at a painting of apple pickers on the wall.

Miss Golding reached a manila folder into one of the many pigeonholes on the desk, then folded her hands primly on her lap. She had a scratch for a smile in an otherwise brooding face.

"You want your children well-prepared to take advantage of the opportunities that present themselves, do you not?" she asked.

Delaney nodded.

"Of course you do." Her greyish hair pulled tight and tied into a bun and her dark brown eyes set close above a sharp nose made for a severe-looking woman. "However, you should understand I have a home here and another in the Annapolis Valley, Mister Delaney, and only a few empty beds. Have I made myself clear?"

Delaney shifted uneasily in the doorway. He looked for some-
place to hide his eyes. He found it in the lion's head carved in
the centre of the rosewood side table. His eyes roved the intricate
carving of the mane and ducked into the shadowy crevices of the
carved wood.

"There is no guarantee you will return," Miss Golding said.
"Joining the army to advance the cause of abolition is noble
indeed. But noble cause or not, Mister Delaney, war takes its toll.
If you want your children to carve out a wholesome place for
themselves in the world, then you must agree that they are mine,
my children to do what is necessary, to do for them what is right,
to mould them into fine men and women, no matter what it
takes and however much time it takes to do."

She turned to the walnut desk and removed a printed document from one of the pigeonholes. She glanced at the document,
then flattened it on the desk. She turned to face Delaney. She
lowered her eyes humbly.

"Suffer the little children to come unto me," she said, "and
forbid them not; for of such is the kingdom of God."

She opened a desk drawer for pen, ink, and blotting paper.
She dipped the pen and positioned the document for Delaney
to sign.

Colley slowed the wagon. Delaney stirred and blinked aside
the memory. Colley stopped at the heavy double doors of a red
brick building with a dozen or so cows corralled beside it. The
three got down from the wagon and Colley hammered on the
double doors.

A slaughterhouse herder in soft cap, bloody coat, and boots
caked with cow shit came out a side door. Colley waved and the
herder went back in and opened the double doors. The tannery
men entered and began carrying fresh skinned hides from a stack
more than six feet high. In no time they had the stack of hides
loaded into the wagon.

The herder led them from the building to an outdoor stack, which reeked from the hides sitting in the sun too long. The tannery men loaded them into the wagon. Then Colley tallied the number of hides in a black notebook. The herder scowled at Colley and reluctantly made his mark.

They climbed on the wagon. Colley drove, and Delaney and Dearborn squeezed on the seat beside him. Colley looked at them, winked, and proudly said, "Letters and numbers. They the keys to the doors white folk don't want us to open."

While unloading hides at the tannery, Colley said to Delaney, "We cook special on Sunday. You come by and meet my family."

Chapter 4

Harley led Sheriff Greene down to the landing. In tall eelgrass they found a dinghy with one oar. There were bloody handprints on the oar and on the gunwale. The handprints were small, a child's. There were footprints in the mud, one set bigger than the other. The prints led up the bank and down river.

Harley and Sheriff Greene poled Harley's raft to the landing on Moose Island and drove it onto the gravel beach, then hauled it up a few feet more and tied it to a birch tree. Not far from the tree, Harley saw where the girls had skidded down over the bank.

"In a hurry, by the look of it," Harley said.

Sheriff Greene pointed to the deep scour line of the dinghy's keel and the churned gravel around it. "Sure looks that way."

The two men climbed the riverbank and crossed a two-acre field, past a horse-drawn mowing machine overgrown with weeds and a hay rake sunk into the unploughed earth. Beyond the field was a small stand of sugar maple, a sagging pole barn, and a rundown, weather-beaten farmhouse with a summer kitchen that leaned and shivered precariously in the wind.

From inside the barn, a cow mooed anxiously and a couple of sheep bleated. Chickens ranged in the farmyard. On the south side of the house was a vegetable garden. The plants had all been gathered. Beyond the garden was an open field in which a horse grazed.

Harley called for Dooley Smith, but there was no answer. He called again and climbed the back porch of the house and called inside. Still no answer.

Sheriff Greene walked to the barn where he found Dooley Smith lying face up just inside the open door. He was dead. His skull was cracked and his brains splattered. A blood-covered fence stake lay on the barn floor beside him.

Harley came up behind Sheriff Greene, took one look at the body and turned away. "Is that Dooley?"

"That's him."

Harley returned for a second look, gagged, and quickly spun around so as not to see. His breathing quickened.

"He's beat up pretty good," Sheriff Greene said without taking his eyes off the corpse. "Beat the lips right off his face."

"Jesus Murphy," Harley said, and choked back his breakfast, which had made its way to his throat.

Sheriff Greene squatted beside the body and rolled it over to see the back of the bashed skull. He figured that was the first blow, from behind. Then he saw a piece of blue cloth under the right shoulder of the body and reached for it. He recognized it right away — a shoulder strap off a blue jumper. He tucked it into a coat pocket. He stood and stepped back a pace and cocked his arms, pretending to swing the fence stake. He imagined Dooley Smith crumbling to his knees, then falling over. The Sheriff's voice fell to a whisper.

"Yeah, he took a beating all right. It didn't stop with him on the ground. Unconscious, maybe, like beating something out of one's self, beating the mind into mindlessness."

"I'm going to be sick," Harley said, and hunched over so as not to splatter himself.

"Be sick outside," the Sheriff ordered, and strode past Harley into the farmyard. "When you're done, feed the livestock and milk the cow. I'm going to look inside the house."

The kitchen was as scrubbed and as tidy as Jenny Pierce's kitchen. Dishes washed and dried on the drain board, tea towel neatly folded, cookstove cleaned and polished, woodbin filled. He lifted a stove lid to see the firebox had burned to ashes.

The parlour appeared unused, so did the small bedroom upstairs. Not so the big bedroom. Here, bed covers were kicked and tangled on the floor. A man's winter jacket and overalls hung on a wall peg beside a young woman's cotton blouse and a younger girl's blue knitted sweater. There was urine in the chamber pot. A wash basin on a washstand was filled with water.

Harley was on the porch when Sheriff Greene came out.

"He was a son of a bitch," Harley said, his face still red from vomiting, his breathing uneven. He rolled his hands over the rickety railing. "But even a son of a bitch don't deserve that."

Sheriff Greene looked past Harley to the barn, then back into the house. He fingered the blue shoulder strap in his pocket. "Are you a churchgoer, Harley?"

"I am."

"Then you know we deserve what we get, every goddamn one of us. Sooner or later we all get what's coming."

Sheriff Greene stepped off the porch and started for the river, stopped at the edge of the field, and looked back over the rundown farm.

"The livestock needs taken care of," he said to Harley, then drew a deep breath and let it out. "Divide them up between you and Jenny Pierce. I think that's fair. I'll send someone for the body. That should settle it."

"What about those girls you said?" Harley pressed.

Sheriff Greene looked where the river pooled beneath an overhanging branch. "Not up to me, Harley. The court will decide on that."

CHAPTER 5

T he tannery stink and that of the boiled bones in the glue yard seeped into Delaney's skin and into his blood. There was no escaping it, not even on a Sunday walk by the river, and not at the young woman's shack where he took tea one time and one time only.

"I suppose Murdock told you about my man?" Maggie asked.

Delaney nodded and sipped his tea.

"He never said he was going, not for good," Maggie said. "He just never came home, not in more than a year. I worked in a stitching mill until Abby come due." She poured herself another cup and one for her mother.

Delaney watched Abby playing on the floor at Maggie's feet.

"Two cups and maybe I'd get more out of you than 'hello' and 'goodbye,'" she said.

Delaney shrugged and drained the last of his tea and leaned down to show Abby a trick with his hands. He pretended his index finger was a stump then blew on his thumb to make his finger pop out.

Maggie tightened her eyes on him, and he felt them and looked up at her. She set her teacup on the table and squared her shoulders in a sort of determined way. "Murdock said he thinks you have a family back home."

Delaney stopped with the hand tricks. He straightened and caught the old woman looking hard at him from her roost beside the stove. He looked at the child at his feet and then at Maggie, who had nervously laced her fingers around the cup.

Delaney stood to go.

Maggie stood as though to challenge him. "I want your time, Arthur Delaney. I got a right to know."

He moved around her to the door. Stood there a moment, then turned to her, his face a specimen of humility. "I got no demands on you. I'm working to keep living, and I'm living to go home. That's all I want. That's everything for me."

He opened the door and stepped out to a blast of cool air. He walked past the barn to the paddock where he leaned over the shabby, horse-cribbed fence and watched the sun disappearing behind the treeline. His mind was heavy with memories, and his heart was consumed with the one desire that had stoked him through every day and every night in that Confederate prison.

Delaney paid half his keep from his tannery wages and the rest he worked off with farm chores. He split and hauled wood for Murray, butchered a calf and salted some of the meat and smoked the rest. He cut what was worth cutting of the hay and salvaged what was salvageable from a field of wheat. Sunday may have been a day of rest, but Delaney took no comfort in that, other than to walk the river before nightfall. Sometimes Murdock Murray walked with him.

"It's not hard to notice, what with you dinnering in the barn," Murray said. "If it's feelings you're hiding from, they show up no matter how well you hide them."

Delaney stooped for a stick that had washed up on the river-bank. He broke off twigs and used it for walking.

"Why we can't bend like the river I'll never know," Murray said.

Delaney tapped with the stick as he walked. "As soon as I put away enough money I'm going home," he said. "I don't want to leave behind a lot of hurt."

"We all have something to make up for," Murray said.

Delaney flung the stick far enough into the river to catch the current.

"Some more than others," Murray said.

"It's a promise I made," Delaney said.

CHAPTER 6

J immy Delaney drove his single bit axe into the trunk of a
tall maple, angling the blade for a downward cut, the way
old Horsnell had taught him how. Sighting it for where
he wanted the tree to drop. He flattened the blade for a hori-
zontal cut, about a foot below the angled one. He kept chopping,
angling the blade then flattening it, until he chopped out a notch
that went deep into the tree. He shifted to the other side of the
tree and came onto it with a series of downward chops, aimed
higher than the notch, but angled to meet it. He chopped a few
more times, then stepped back and to one side. With the axe
handle, he nudged the tree to fall. It landed where he had planned
it would.

Sixteen and already filled out like a man, doing man's work
for a hard-luck Stewiacke farmer. An unpaid hired hand working
into the second year of a three-year bond that Miss Golding,
the head of Hillside Farm Orphanage and Refuge Centre, had

negotiated with Rufus DeWolfe. He knew what he was, another man's property, a slave in his own mind, doing whatever DeWolfe and his haggard wife ordered him to do.

He set the axe against the fallen tree and drank from a wooden canteen. He listened to the woods. To birdsong and the scurry of small animals. To the sound of his own breathing and to the silent trace of thoughts no one could prevent him from having. Thoughts of a faraway place of his own, in a grassland that was vast and open the way old Horsnell had said it was, an unshackled land where there was nothing, nothing to stop the eye from seeing.

He pulled a stone from his pocket and sharpened the axe blade. Still dreaming of that place, of taking his chances out there somewhere.

He got up and limbed the tree and cleared the slash from underfoot. With a bucksaw he sawed the trunk into logs for milling into boards. The limbs he sawed into stove wood.

It was coming on dark when he finished the chopping and sawing. He carried the axe over one shoulder and slung the bucksaw over the other. He walked humming a tune that had been in and out of his head for as long as he could remember. He could hear his mother's voice singing words he did not understand, but shaping images of a time he sensed was his.

He soon cleared the woods to an open field. The sky was filled with stars, flocks of them, cold in their distance, yet, as old Horsnell had said of them, beacons to sailors and wayfarers. Learn them and you won't get lost, Horsnell had advised. Hard not to feel lost to the dreams he had. Talking them out to himself. Not lonely, even though most of his time he spent alone. Eager was more like it. Eager to live his dreams into his life. Sixteen and feeling the need to get on with it.

He walked across the muddy farmyard and leaned the axe and saw against the side wall of the woodshed in which he lived.

His bed was in a corner between the stacks. A bowl of porridge had been left for him on a chopping block. A stale hunk of bread beside it. He ate hungrily, washing the bread down with water from his canteen.

CHAPTER 7

‧❦‧

E arly Sunday morning Arthur Delaney walked to Colley's
place to help him harvest a crop of oats before winter.
The tree-lined road to Colley's veered off the Great
Pennsylvania Wagon Road and dipped into a hollow beside a
shallow stream with a cobble bottom. Straddling the stream was a
hamlet of log houses and outbuildings. Colley's was the house set
farthest back from the stream, and beyond that was a field that ran
along the base of a low hill. A fieldstone wall divided the field:
one quarter for pasture, the rest in hay.

Dearborn was there, along with another man named Roberts.
The four of them had the field scythed before mid-morning.
With the sun now high and hot, the men removed their shirts
before raking the hay for drying. Delaney saw the thick scars on
Dearborn and Roberts's backs. He knew the how of it. Snake
whip in a cotton field for working slow or for hollering a song to

tenderize the work. He saw the same whip in a prison yard for mooching food or missing roll call.

Dearborn had put up a batch of beer. After raking hay the men sat in the shade of an old oak and drank a bit while they waited for the hay to dry. They talked and watched a group of children playing in an open area among the houses, playing a game they had learned from Union soldiers during the war. It involved a hide-covered ball and a tapered stick. Dearborn and Roberts walked over to play this new game with the children.

Dearborn picked up the tapered stick and cocked it over his shoulder as he had seen the Union soldiers do. One of the children pitched him the ball. Dearborn swung the stick, missed the ball, and tied himself up in knots. Roberts took a turn and fared no better than Dearborn.

Delaney and Colley stayed sitting under the tree. They watched the men and children playing. Then Delaney told Colley how he used to chase Robina, Jimmy, and Annie around their three-room house on Tulip Street, where he had lived. Him swelling his shoulders and growling like a wild beast, and the three kids squealing and running every which way to escape his grasp.

The memory dragged him into a sad silence. Colley saw it and said he would buy a penny's worth of Delaney's thoughts if it would help.

Delaney stood and shoved his hands into his pockets and turned toward the field they had scythed. After a while he turned back to Colley.

"Jimmy I could've done for," he said, "but the girls, not without a mother. What did I know about stitching and darning, and about Robina ripening into a woman? Nothing at all. I knew nothing about the questions the girls would have one day, and even less about the answers they would need to hear."

He leaned his back against the oak and slowly slid down to his haunches.

"Easy giving in to the talk about abolition," he said. "Easy joining up. Easy giving my children to the promises Miss Golding made."

He told Colley about following Nelly McIvor and Bessie Morris to the Mechanics Hall to hear temperance talk and a lecture by Miss Emma Golding on "the need to protect our children."

The Hall was in a small wood-frame building. It had a raised stage, proscenium arch, and a thick purple curtain with a satin sheen. There was a podium at the front of the stage and behind this, against the closed curtain, were four straight-back chairs. One each for the chairman and vice-chairman of the Mechanics Institute, one for Douglas Currie, the director of the Christian Charitable and Temperance Union, and one for Miss Emma Golding, the founder and director of the Children's Refuge and Aid Home in Halifax.

The temperance talk by Douglas Currie was all table-thumping and Bible-waving against the evils of drink. Then the Chairman introduced Miss Emma Golding. She stood awkwardly and limped to the podium. Her black floor-length dress all but hid the six-inch heel that made up for her right leg being shorter than her left. Upon reaching the podium, she was quick to silence the stirring tones among those uncomfortable at seeing a well-born lady limp.

"Suffer the little children to come unto me," she said.

Her rounded voice brimmed with confidence, and her arms opened wide from her hefty bosom to include all who sat before her. She told how that particular passage from the Gospel of St. Matthew had started her caring for God's children. She opened an orphanage in Scotland, and soon enough one orphanage became two, and two grew to four. She fed, clothed, housed, schooled, and attended the medical needs of more than three hundred children at any given time.

Miss Golding lowered her eyes humbly and waited for the silence to work in the hearts of her listeners. Then she released her hands from the podium and limped to the forward edge of the stage, closing the distance between herself and her audience. She raised a closed fist to her lips, held it a moment as though kissing something she held and cherished. Then she lowered it. Her eyes fixed all in the room by fixing those sitting at the centre.

To Arthur Delaney, she was looking straight at him.

"The work is hardly done," she said, and unfolded her arms to gesture to the world beyond the shiplap walls. Her voice lowered to a whisper, which could still be heard in the back row. It climbed slowly as she spoke, like a bird on an updraft of warm air.

"There are more, many more children who need my protection, care, and schooling. This is why I have crossed the Atlantic to open a home here in Halifax, and another, a working farm for older children, at Aylesford in the Annapolis Valley. There are children here whose bellies starve for crumbs and whose hearts hunger for love. For the sake of Christ Almighty, I seek to give them the chance to find their rightful place in the world, the chance to achieve a bright and fruitful future. Suffer the little children to come unto me, and forbid them not; for of such is the kingdom of God."

Colley tipped the half-keg of beer for another taste.

"I stood and clapped with everyone else," Delaney said. "The next day I went to see her."

Colley looked at Delaney. "No family to care for your children?"

"In Ireland," Delaney said. "Mine and Mary's. We came over from Ennis. Left everything, except my tools: saws and planes and chisels."

Colley thought for a moment, face strained, then he said, "Children make up for the lows in our lives. I had none during slave times. Now me and Bergie making up for it." He smiled happily.

Delaney smiled with him, then pointed to Dearborn hitching his draft horse to a hay rick. Roberts threw forks into the rick, then hopped on board to ride to the far side of the scythed field. Colley and Delaney got up and walked behind the rick.

"My wife has clothes that would fit you better than what you're wearing," Colley said. "Her brother's clothes. He joined a Free Slave regiment and got himself killed at Milliken's Bend in Louisiana. Unless you mind wearing them."

Delaney thanked him, and said, "I was the bone-picker in prison. I know about wearing dead men's clothes."

CHAPTER 8

S heriff Greene led Annie through a stone archway and into a vault with two jail cells. Sheriff Greene towered over the twelve-year-old girl, who slunk behind with her shoulders rolled forward and her grim face buried in fear.

A man with a long black beard and steely blue eyes was in one of the cells. Robina was already in the other. Both prisoners sat on their bunks. Both wore leg irons.

On seeing Annie, Robina got up and clanked forward and gripped the bars with both hands. Annie placed her hands over Robina's and tried for a smile.

Sheriff Greene unlocked the bearded man's cell and led him from the vault to an outer office. He returned and slid a wooden bench from the far end of the vault and positioned it in front of Robina's cell, close to the iron bars.

"Not much longer," he said, and left the sisters to themselves.

Annie sat on the bench, then quickly got up and reached both arms through the bars to hug Robina. Robina hugged her back. They unclenched and stared lovingly at each other.

Slowly Robina surfaced from the murk deep inside herself. She drew back and offered Annie a twilight smile and said, "I'll be going away from here. The penitentiary in Saint John."

"I know," Annie said.

They hugged and kissed and cried. Through her tears Robina said, "We'll find our way, Annie. I promise."

After a while, Sheriff Greene returned and told Annie it was time for her to go. "The Clooneys are waiting to take you home," he said.

Robina drew away from the bars and sat on the bunk. Her shoulders sank and her arms went limp to see Annie walk from the vault.

Outside the York County Jail a baggy-eyed woman waited in a horse-drawn open carriage. A whiskered man sat in the driver's seat.

Sheriff Greene offered Annie his hand for her to get in.

She hesitated. Her shoulders stiff and unwilling.

"You have to go with them," the Sheriff said. "It's a court order."

Annie got in the carriage and sat forward on the seat. It was clear she was anxious about her situation.

The whiskered man snapped the reins, and the carriage threw up dust.

CHAPTER 9

I t was near midnight when he woke to the barn door opening.
A pale light chased the shadows into the dark corners of the
barn. Delaney tensed and balled his fists the way he had done
in prison when the guards had made late-night rounds. He reached
for the carving knife. Slowly he stood and pressed his body flat
against the cribbed wood of the horse stall. He gripped the carving
knife and strained to see around a post. He saw Maggie standing in
lantern light in what seemed a loose weave of white linen.

"Maggie?"

She turned to his voice and gave a smile that slowly and sadly
melted from her face. She broke out crying and crumbled into
his arms.

"I need you," she begged. "Murdock's off in town and I
need help."

They left the barn and hurried across the farmyard in silence;
Maggie gripped by grief, Delaney strung tight by what he knew

awaited him in Maggie's one-room shack. The night air was dank with the smell of wet fallen leaves, and with corn stalks blackened by frost.

He picked up pebbles and led Maggie into the shack and to the bed by the stove where Abby lay tucked and tangled in the bedclothes. "You just settle in with her," he said. "I'll do what needs doing."

The old woman sat slumped in the rocker, her jaw unhinged and her eyes rolled back in her head. Carefully, almost reverently, he lifted the old woman from the rocker. She felt heavier than his wife, Mary, had felt when he had lifted her to the table for washing. He laid the old woman out on the bed that was propped on wooden blocks and leaning against the back wall of the shack. He straightened the old woman's threadbare dress, closed her eyes with the pebbles he had picked up in the farmyard, pulled the plaid shawl from around her shoulders, and used it to tie up her fallen jaw. He turned to Maggie, who was watching him.

"In the morning I'll fetch a midwife to wash and dress her for burial," he said.

He blew out the light and sat in the rocker. From somewhere outside Maggie's shack, he heard what he had heard when keeping vigil for his wife, the death-watch ticking down to an unwound silence. He remembered soaking a grey rag in vinegar and water, and washing Mary's neck. The skin that he had often kissed seemed altogether strange. Stranger still had been the weight of her bony body when he had rolled it to wash her arms, which waved as though waving goodbye, then her legs and feet.

Even now he could hear Nelly McIvor telling him how to prepare the dead for burial. Nelly had been miffed at his insistence on doing it. She stirred restless at the loving way he patted and smoothed the rag over the bruises on his wife's right thigh and hip. "The marks of death," Nelly had said. "They don't rub out."

He raised his wife's head and squeezed the rag over it. The water had run down her face like tears. It dripped from her chin and through the sunken hollows, which had been her breasts. Then he washed under her arms and where she had soiled herself in dying.

Abby whimpered in her sleep, and he turned to see Maggie draw the child closer to her body for comfort, the way Mary had done on winter nights when all three, Robina, Jimmy, and Annie, had snuggled in the big bed together, sharing her motherly warmth, all sixty pounds of her if there was an ounce, coughing and choking day and night, and shaking through his arms and into his heart.

"Promise," Mary had begged the night before she had died.

He had nodded, but for Mary a nod was not enough. She had needed the full weight of his words. So she made him say it, with his hand on her heart.

"I promise," he had said and dropped his eyes and kissed her hands. "I promise."

He stopped rocking to hear the rustle of Abby shifting in her mother's arms and then the two of them breathing with the same steady breath. He longed to join them, to pace his breathing to their rhythm, to sleep beside them until morning, or for an hour; if not an hour, then a moment, a single moment asleep in someone's arms, without regret.

He hung his head and sat in the rocker for the longest time. Then he stood and slowly crossed the room to the window. He pressed his forehead against the cool glass. He lifted his eyes and allowed his mind to follow moonlight up the quiet road; the road that he knew he was bound to travel, the road that would return him home, the road that somehow would break beneath him like a wave.

CHAPTER 10

Mid-November, and a north wind blew a cold snap across Pennsylvania. Into Murray's farmyard that same wind blew a tightly built man riding a brown sway-back mare. The man wore a grey duster snugged up to his chin and a blue slouch hat pulled low against the wind.

From beside the woodpile and chopping block, Delaney watched the man slowly ride up to Maggie's shack, dismount, and go inside. He heard Maggie squeal happily and the man grunt something that Delaney could not make out.

Murdock Murray stood at his open front door looking to catch Delaney's eye. When Delaney looked at him, Murray nodded and Delaney knew at once that the man was Maggie's man, Billy Woods. He also knew by the way Billy Woods swaggered into Maggie's shack that he'd be staying for a while.

Delaney finished his chopping and carried an armload to the main house. "Darkness coming on," he said.

"More than you know with him coming here. He throws his weight around," Murray said, scooping a plate of boiled potatoes and boiled beef from a pot at the back of the stove. He passed Delaney the plate. "Gets his way like he does. Mean and meaner when he gets drinking. Backs himself up with a wheel gun."

Delaney carried his plate to the door. "I'll keep my distance," he said.

Murray held a lantern as they walked to the barn. "Two cocks in a henhouse are bound to tangle," he said.

They entered the barn and Delaney set the plate on the top rail of a stall. He took a light off Murray's lantern and struck another lantern that was hanging from a post peg. "I understand," he said. The light filled his face, and he knew it showed his disappointment.

"It's hard travelling in winter," Murray said. "But you'll be better served if you did."

Delaney sat down on the harness, spooned a mouthful, and chewed.

"It breaks me to say that," Murray said, his voice warbling with shame. "But I'm too old and weak to stand my ground." He leaned his back against the post. "There have been others nosing around."

"I seen them." Delaney spooned another mouthful. "Are they with him?"

Murray shook his head. "Local boys. Who knows what is stirring them up."

Delaney looked kindly at Murray. "Will this fellow help you around the farm?"

Again Murray shook his head. The lantern light shimmered in his white hair. "He's nothing but a taker. He run down escaped slaves before the war. During it he rode with Mosely's rangers. Thieves was what they were."

Delaney finished eating and handed Murray the empty plate. He started packing his belongings into his bedroll: the carving knife, wooden doll, cracked mirror, money pouch. He got up and removed a faded photograph from the side of the stall where he had pinned it with a sliver of wood.

Murray craned his neck to see the photograph.

"My family," Delaney said, and his eyes glazed at the memory of standing at a copper sink in a room at the back of Richard Stayner's house in Halifax, standing in the glow from a lamp covered with a red cloth. Stayner, a tall man bent at the waist for the low ceiling, dipped two glass plates into gallic acid and set them aside to dry.

"We will give it time," Stayner had said. "Just watch."

Slowly, ghostly shapes appeared on the glass plates. Delaney saw himself sitting beside his wife in a double-seat arrow back rocker. He was holding her upright, so gently, as though her wasted body would fall apart in his arms.

Robina and Annie stood at their mother's side, their heads angled toward hers. Both were dressed for Sunday. Robina was eight, all elbows and knees and beaming. Annie, a five-year-old, with dark hair cut short in the shape of a bowl, touched the lacy bib on her mother's dark-coloured dress. Jimmy, nearly eleven, pressed his hip against his father's side of the chair, his face thrust forward, almost defiant.

In the starkness of the photographic image, Mary Delaney looked like someone who was already dead.

"A handsome family," Murray said.

Delaney carefully placed the cardboard-backed photograph into his bedroll. "I carried it all these years. Protected it."

"The morning would've been soon enough to leave," Murray said.

As Delaney rolled his bedding tight and cinched it with leather straps, he said, "I don't want trouble for you. I'll bed down at Wendell Colley's tonight. I appreciate what you done for me."

Murrray told Delaney to wait and he went up to the house and came back. He offered Delaney a knee-length sheepskin coat.

"I've had that for a while," he said. "There was more to me back then. It might go a little tight on you, but a hide coat always got some give."

Delaney accepted the coat without fuss and pulled it on. He strung his bedroll across his shoulders and reached for Murray's hand.

Murray offered him a lantern to light his way along the road to Colley's place, but Delaney refused to take it, saying he knew the road well enough and that a sky full of stars offered plenty of light.

Delaney had no sooner walked from the farmyard to the road than he heard Maggie Francis scream from her shack. He bolted from the road and across the farmyard. Murray dropped the plate and ran behind and caught up with Delaney outside the shack.

Maggie shrieked again, and then again.

Delaney pushed the door open and stepped inside. Murray entered with him, holding up the lantern. In its light they saw Billy Woods standing in the middle of the room, naked. Maggie was in bed, a bolster pulled up to her chin. Abby lay on the cot facing the outside wall, whimpering.

Woods reached down to his trousers on the floor and came up with a Colt single action revolver, what Murray had called a "wheel gun." He aimed it at Delaney.

Murray quickly backed from the shack and stood several steps to one side of the open door. The room went shadowy dark. Threads of lantern light slipped through the cracks between the wallboards. One of them glinted off the revolver in Woods's hand. Another fell across the bed in which Maggie lay.

Delaney could no longer see Woods's face, but he sensed it, the meanness in it, and the coldness of it, like the cold steel of the gun six feet between them. He heard Maggie stirring in the bed. She cried for him to get out. Then she groaned from a hollow deep inside.

Delaney stood his ground. Then he heard the distinct click of the hammer being cocked, and he trembled with the chill that swept over him. He held his breath, as though holding it would keep Billy Woods from pulling the trigger.

Again Maggie cried for him to go.

"I'm going," Delaney said on an intake of air. He swallowed hard. "I am going."

He slowly turned his back to the gun and to the man holding it, and to the woman in the bed and the child on the cot, and just as slowly he stepped from the shack and closed the door behind.

"I'll walk you to the road," Murray said. "Walk out the jitters in my legs."

Chapter 11

For Jimmy, November was for chunking up firewood, loading the farm wagon, and selling the loads in Truro. A week of chopping and hauling and Jimmy got himself too tired to sleep. One night he lay in his bunk listening to DeWolfe and his wife arguing outside their house, arguing the way drunks do, incoherently, seeming to have no nub to what they were arguing about. Jimmy got up and opened the shed door.

In spill light from the house, he saw DeWolfe with his chin thrust forward, snarling. And DeWolfe's rail-thin wife, her mouth going a mile a minute, screaming in her high-pitched voice. It sounded like a knife blade on a grindstone. After a while, Jimmy realized they were arguing about money, and how much it cost to keep him on, and how much Robert Child would pay for Jimmy to work for him.

Jimmy slipped from the shed and ran across the field for the treeline. He knew what usually came next. DeWolfe would argue himself crazy, stumble around in the muddy yard, then charge into the shed with the ash stick he used for herding cows and beat Jimmy until the boy ran from the shed. No reason. Just anger, and the need to beat the anger out on someone else.

Three times that had happened. After that, whenever Jimmy heard DeWolfe arguing with his wife, he rolled billets of wood into his bedroll and made himself scarce. He sat with his back against a tree and listened for DeWolfe to rip into the shed and beat the hell out of his bedroll. Usually that was enough to quell the farmer's foul mood, enough that he would return to the house, slump on a kitchen chair, and fall asleep. That night, however, DeWolfe fetched a lantern and walked the road to Robert Child's house.

Come morning, Jimmy found out why. DeWolfe had negotiated half his bond with Robert Child.

Two farms, each with half of Jimmy's bond, each demanding all of his labour. For two weeks, Jimmy worked for both of them. He chopped, split, and hauled for Rufus DeWolfe. At the same time he knocked down spruce trees and twitched them from the woods for building a pole barn for Robert Child. He worked himself to exhaustion.

On Sunday morning, DeWolfe led his plough horse from the paddock beside the barn, hitched it to the wagon Jimmy used for hauling wood, climbed his wife aboard, and drove to the Methodist Church to pray their way into Christ's good grace.

That same morning Jimmy packed a lumberman's shirt, and a whetstone and steel into his bedroll. With the axe over his shoulder, he followed the treeline to an old Mi'kmaq path that led to the Shubenacadie River. The path ran along the riverbank, and soon widened into a road the drovers used for herding livestock to market in Halifax. He walked lightly, humming and talking to himself. He planned out his life over one mile, then changed it during the next. No fear for what lay around the bend. Eager for it to unfold into a day that was all his.

He walked at a pace that landed him at Grand Lake before nightfall. He cut spruce boughs for a bed and a lean-to, and gathered deadfall for a fire. He banked the fire with stones to reflect the heat into the lean-to. Lying in his bedroll, his skin sensed the stillness of the lake and noisy quiet of the woods behind. He searched the night sky for the dipper and the North Star, and the Archer and the Bull. He hoped for a shooting star to make a wish on. He fell asleep no more hungry than usual.

He woke to a cold and grey day, which hurried him to pack his bedroll and get going. A fingerboard pointed the way to Halifax. Before long, he fell in with a cloth and ribbon peddler named John Dinan. The twenty miles passed easily. Dinan was jolly by nature, and talkative. Happy for the young man's company, willing to share his food and his far-fetched stories, which he told one after another. About sea monsters and ghost ships, and about Peter Coop, a Mi'kmaq hunter, who shot and wounded a bear, then tracked it into thick under-brush, where the bear charged and grabbed Coop in its fatal hug and squeezed.

"The bear damn near broke that Indian in half," Dinan said. He set his pack on the ground and sat beside it.

Jimmy remained standing, his eyes wide for Dinan to finish telling.

Dinan smiled and looked straight at Jimmy.

"Peter Coop was three breaths short of dying," the peddler said. "But he plucked up and reached into the bear's mouth, grabbed its tongue, and held on until that bear strangled to death."

Dinan flattened one hand out and held up the other as though swearing an oath on a stack of Bibles.

Jimmy shook his head in disbelief. Dinan reached into his pack and held up what he said were Peter Coop's canvas pants, "with the arse clawed out."

Dinan laughed and Jimmy laughed, and the two marched on

to Halifax. They camped on the Dartmouth side of the harbour, near a Mi'kmaq village at Turtle Cove.

"I once lived not too far from here," Jimmy said. He watched Dinan slip a gutted codfish onto cross sticks and jam the sticks between rocks before an open fire. Two days together on the road and this was the first time Jimmy had said anything telling about himself.

"A cottage on Tulip Street," Jimmy continued, poking at the flames with a stick. Thinking into the fire. "Up from the Slips, a shipyard where my father worked. Robina and me would sit on a hill and watch a schooner grow. Hundreds of men, and us picking him out, sawing and hammering. We sometimes waited for quitting time to walk him home."

Jimmy stopped talking. Dinan tested the flakiness of the fish. He halved it on a flat stone and scrapped Jimmy's share onto a tin plate.

"Is your family still there?" he chanced to ask, eating his share off the stone.

Jimmy fingered a mouthful of fish. "Sisters is all I got," he said, chewing. "Robina and Annie."

Dinan speared a potato with a sharp stick and gave it to Jimmy. He speared another.

"Mother and father?" Dinan asked.

Jimmy shook his head. "My mother died and that bitch of a Miss Golding said my father got killed."

"Working in the shipyard?"

Again Jimmy shook his head, this time slowly, lips pursed. "Soldiering at somewhere I don't know. I told Robina I don't believe none of it."

Dinan ate and listened.

Jimmy talked as he chewed. "Miss Golding. She called us down, and we sat outside her office. She ran the home. She separated the boys from the girls, so my sisters and me never talked.

We saw one another, but not to talk. Sitting there was the first time in months."

Jimmy went silent for a while, then continued. "Robina said her and Annie and the other girls were scrubbing walls and floors in rich people's homes, laundering and ironing their clothes. She said we were all going to a farm."

He stared at the fire without eating. He set his plate on a rock beside him. "I don't want to talk no more," he said. He got up and walked away from the fire. He looked at the scattering of lights across the harbour. He remembered sitting with his sisters on the boot bench outside Miss Golding's office, and Robina saying she missed their mother and father, that Annie still cried herself to sleep most nights, and that she would hug Jimmy tight, tight if he would let her. He had shaken Robina's arms from around his shoulders. Begrudged her what he was feeling. Wishing he hadn't.

Then MacDonald, the overseer, as thin and straight as a candle, had pointed him down a small hallway to a green door to the scullery.

"MacDonald does the caning," Angus Jennings, the head boy, had said. He handed Jimmy a blue smock. "Miss Golding hates boys."

"When my father comes . . ."

"He won't come. None of them do."

Jimmy returned to the fire and gnawed on the hot potato. Silent. Unwilling to look at John Dinan. Uncomfortable with what he had already said.

༄

Early the following morning, they walked past the Dartmouth Slips to the waterfront. Jimmy craned to see the ship being built.

"Two-mast schooner," Jimmy said, pointing. "Near three hundred ton. A Grand Banker. Be rigged for fishing."

"You know ships," Dinan said.

"Not much more than what my father said."

Dinan asked if Jimmy wanted to walk up around Tulip Street, and Jimmy said, "No. The dead live there."

At the waterfront, Dinan tipped a ferryman to row them across to Halifax. Once on the water, the wind picked up, blowing out of the northwest, blowing over the water a choke-drawn stink of boiled fat and chimney smoke, as well as the low murmur of voices, hundreds of them. From the bow of the dory, Jimmy looked out on a forest of ship masts on the waterfront, and then wood-frame buildings climbing the steep hill to the stone fortress at the top.

"The city saw prosperous times while the Yanks fought each other," Dinan said. "Both sides were sinking ships like shooting pigeons out on the back commons. I for one wanted that war to never end."

The dory landed on the beach beside the Queen's Wharf. Draymen shouldered their carts from the waterfront and up the hill. Their high boots splashed in the runoff and mud. The waterfront was a hustle of men, in different-coloured woollen caps. They were stevedoring cargo on and off ships that were tied up at the wharfs, and off tenders that had pulled to shore from ships anchored toward the narrows end of the harbour.

"We rowed across hardly ever," Jimmy said, as they walked in the crowd along the waterfront, past Shippy's Tavern, where sailors hung from the door, pissing off last night's drunk. They walked past a fold of steamy sheep beside Blagrave's Inn, past a rickety-legged woman drawing water from a trough that ran down from a pump on Pleasant Street, past a scatter of dried lumber and a chandler's shop and a tinker's stall.

They said their goodbyes and went their ways: Dinan to stock up his wares at a haberdasher on Spring Garden Road, and Jimmy to look for work at a sprawling market under a pavilion off Bedford Row.

Horses steamed and stamped in the mud. Their smell mingled with those of fish flakes and the dressed carcasses of fly-blown meat. Near a butcher's stall a toothless woman, bundled in a soldier's greatcoat and with a red bandana on her head, leaned against one of the plain oak pillars that held up the pavilion roof. A child squatted in the sawdust and blood at the woman's feet. The child gawked at the blotch of faces surrounding her.

Jimmy asked the woman about finding work. She shrugged and shook her head. He asked the butcher, who ignored him. He walked through the market asking for work and finding none.

A man standing at a stall stocked with turnip and potatoes clutched his chest and staggered and fell. Jimmy stared at him lying in the mud and sawdust, until a crowd gathered around the man. Someone brought a wheelbarrow. Two others helped him load the stricken man into it. Jimmy watched as they carted the man away.

He looked at faces. Some dirty, others split at the seams, still others worn and chafed, like dried leather gloves.

He neared the meat sellers and fishmongers. Livestock mooed, baaed, and cackled. The fly-filled air smelled of dried blood and scales. Knives gleamed and flashed through red flesh and white. Whole cod, racked like dead soldiers after a fight, stared emptily at the passersby who sniffed the gills for freshness.

At a fish stall, the monger directed Jimmy toward the harbour mouth and a cobble beach where fish shacks were at the end of long, wooden wharves. He pointed to a shallop and said it was sailing that way.

"Tell Darcy to sail you to Henneberry's for work," he said.

Jimmy did and before long he was on board the shallop under sail, gliding toward open water, farther away from Rufus DeWolfe and Robert Child, and from Miss Golding sitting erect at her pigeonhole desk, holding up what she had called official correspondence, rotating toward him and his sisters, a slit for a smile, telling them their father had been shot dead in that war he ran away to.

CHAPTER 12

D elaney said his goodbyes to Colley and his wife and asked Colley to look in on Murdock Murray once in a while. He set off for a two-day tramp from Gurdy's Run to Bradley Junction, to catch an eastbound train.

Train travel to Philadelphia and then on to New York City had Delaney scraping the bottom of his money pouch. He walked the wooden sidewalks down Broadway to Wall Street and then struck out on the snow-covered Post Road through the Bronx and Yonkers, ending up in New Haven, Connecticut.

With what little money he had left, he let a room at the back of a red brick, four-storey tenement on Ferry Street, near the Quinnipiac River. Come morning, he traipsed the New Haven streets begging for work wherever he could. The boss of a rail gang offered him a job, clearing track for the horse-drawn trolleys. One day led to two and two to three, and then Delaney was back on the street searching for work.

Outside Adam and Taylor's warehouse on Chapel Street, a former soldier saw Delaney's beat-up kepi and suggested he try Krall's Coal Company. The company needed a few men with strong backs. Delaney landed the job barrowing sacks of coal to downtown shops and offices along New Haven's ice- and mud-rutted streets.

He held that job for five weeks, then packed his duffle and made for Boston. He was three days walking the Post Road, which was busy with pedestrians and sleighs near the towns and villages, but long and lonely between them. He slept in a chicken coop one night, tucking himself in a corner. The following night he slept in a haymow in an open field, tucking his tired bones into the mound of hay to keep warm.

In the morning he crawled from the hay to see that it had snowed all night and was still snowing. He looked over the white landscape, which seemed suspended in time. The walking was slow but fanciful, with flakes blowing in the balsam and hemlock, and rippling over a field and drifting against snake fences and stone walls.

A sleigh came by and stopped a short distance ahead. The driver, bundled in a fur coat and hat, waved for Delaney to join him.

The driver said he was a doctor who had spent all night with a patient. Delaney swept the ice from his beard and from his eyelids and said he was a soldier returning home.

"Winter has been too long," the doctor said.

"Cold," Delaney said.

"Yes. Cold and . . . Cold and shivering."

Delaney hunched into his sheepskin coat as though the word shivering made him feel even colder.

They sleighed for a while through pine woods heavy with snow. Then the doctor asked about him. Delaney repeated what he had told others: that he had fought for the Union side and was now going home to his children. The doctor asked about his wife and Delaney told him that she had died.

"I served as well," the doctor said. "A field hospital in the Army of the Potomac." He looked off and said something that got lost in the squeak and jangle of the sleigh and the sweep of its runners and in the horse steaming on an upgrade.

"You would think a doctor would get used to it," the doctor said. "Gettysburg. Antietam." He shook his head. "Last night, a thirteen-year-old boy was dying hour by hour. The father outside walking circles around the house. The mother already burning the Christmas greens. Throwing them to the fire. She kept asking me, shovelling the ashes and asking me, whose fault?"

Delaney looked into the man's tired eyes.

"If we don't blame God, then who do we blame?" the doctor asked.

"I don't know," Delaney said, uncomfortable with the doctor speaking so openly. "I don't know who to blame."

"We all looked away for an instant, and our world became a slaughterhouse," the doctor said.

Delaney flinched and looked off through a stand of white birch to see woodmen chopping trees.

The doctor firmly gripped the reins, slowing the horse on the downhill.

"What about you?" he asked. "Are you to blame?"

Delaney did not look at him.

They sleighed in silence for a mile or more. Up ahead there were roofs glittering with frost, and black chimney smoke. The doctor brought the sleigh to a stop at a crossroad. Delaney got out.

"The heart plunges," the doctor said, and flicked the reins for the horse to turn down the crossroad.

CHAPTER 13

I n Boston, with what little money remained, Delaney splurged on a shared room in Sullivan's boarding house on the south side of the city. The following day he looked for work at the Charleston Shipyard. Carpenters the shipyard had plenty of. Delaney hired on as a labourer unloading lumber from a barge in the harbour. The job lasted two days, which paid for his lodging and meals for a few nights.

After supper, Mrs. Sullivan stopped him outside the dining room and handed him a message a child had delivered that afternoon: *8 o'clock. Side Door. No. 5 Tremont Street.*

Mrs. Sullivan had read the message because she commented when she handed it to him, "And here you are shouldering up with the fancies in this city." She said it loud enough for those boarders still at the table to hear.

"Privileged." Delaney heard someone say as he left the boarding house to do what he had done the night before: walk the evening away by letting his feet take him just anywhere. He turned a corner and remembered what Murdock Murray had said about "just anywhere," being just around the bend. He turned into an alley, attracted by a fire and the voices of a group of Irishmen standing around it. They shifted from one foot to the other, scuffing the ground with their heavy feet in clumsy shoes. Their shadows hulked across the alley and up the sides of surrounding three-storey tenements, monstrous in firelight. Delaney joined them and listened to their gripes and complaints mumbled over the flames. Heads nodded in agreement or in sorrow.

One of the men fed a board to the fire and it flamed and snapped sparks. In the flared light, Delaney saw faces worn thin like old cloth, and faces stretched with worry for the hard times that had followed the war. There were other faces frightened of the battle-crazed memories they could not stop from seeing.

Anyone looking at him would have seen his face every bit as frightened as the others. His unsettled eyes watery for the soldiers he had buried in the prison graveyard, and for the drummer boy in the prison's cellar, dead for days, and him grabbing the boy under one shoulder to carry him out for burial and feeling his thumb press through the boy's papery skin.

One man stood humbly before the fire, head bowed to the flames as if in prayer. Another was wizened looking, and shivering despite the heat. He held his balance on the arm of another man who wore a round hat, which sat on the crown of his head. Several others wore the remnants of army uniforms or hand-me-downs from the better sort.

The firelight danced in the glassy eyes of a man with a red beard. The amber light deepened the weathered colour of his face and hands. Others knew him and one of them called out, "O'Connell, give us a song."

O'Connell threw back his shoulders and grieved a song for a young seafarer wrecked on the rocky shoals off Cape St. Ann.

Delaney and several others sang the chorus, about the sad-eyed colleen awaiting his return. The song fell off to a long silence.

Two men joined those around the fire. One of them had a crooked nose and weepy eyes. He wore a tattered brown overcoat. Someone called him Noah Harte.

The other one wore a Union army cap. He grinned and raised his right arm and said, "Faugh an Bhealach."

Delaney heard it and studied the two men as though he expected to know them. "Faugh an Bhealach" — "Clear the Way" — was the battle cry of the 28th Massachusetts Volunteers, Delaney's old regiment. Before the man lowered his arm, Delaney saw the man was missing a thumb and two fingers. The same man who had called Noah Harte by name now said this man was Shamus Tombs.

From inside his brown overcoat, Noah Harte pulled a jug, took a swig, and passed it around. He had something to say and rose to his full height to say it.

"We fought a war and won nothing for ourselves," he said.

A few grumbled in agreement. Most simply stared at the tall man who talked as much with his hands as with his voice.

"We're slaves, every Irish one of us," he continued. "We've been slaves for how many hundred years. No war to free us. Puzzle me the answer to that."

Some men lowered their heads. Others looked to someone else to reply. No one did.

Shamus Tombs swallowed hard and said, "Money owed for fighting and no work when we come home."

"Jobs there are," Noah Harte added, "but not for Irish, not for us." He pointed at Tombs. "The money owed us goes south. Reconstruction they call it. Our money paying those Negroes and Johnny Reb soldiers to work our jobs."

The jug made its way back to Noah Harte and he tucked it under his overcoat. He said, "All that fighting, and we got nothing out of it except freed slaves coming here and working our work for less than we can work it for."

Tombs leaned toward the fire, his face orange in the glow. "And we're paying for it. Our families go hungry, and down south our government is paying our bonus money to the likes of them, paying them to build back what we marched on and tore down."

The man holding his balance on another man's arm grumbled that soldiering was the only job he ever could get, and now he can't work or live normally because of it.

The man in the round hat said, "It's the way of things, that's all."

Tombs responded, "Don't have to be."

The man in the round hat shrugged.

Harte said, "There are hundreds of Irish, hundreds like us willing to fight for our rights. Army rifles and ammunition and then we march."

"March where?" the man in the round hat pressed.

"Where we need to march, where someone will listen."

Delaney ducked under a coil of smoke and stepped back from the firelight.

"Bugle blast and drum beat," O'Connell angrily challenged. "Streams of blood." He glared at Harte and Tombs. "Haven't you had enough fighting?"

Noah Harte made a calming gesture with his hands and said, "You fought to free slaves, but you won't fight to free our own."

"Bullets and bayonets," O'Connell cried at them. "Metal on bone. Words for it are hopeless. Look at us. Look in our eyes. The wildness is gone."

Delaney looked at the men around the fire and saw what O'Connell said was true. Disheartened men with faces rigid from the afterimages of battle.

"Beat your drum elsewhere," O'Connell said.

"The mud is never thicker than this," Harte said, and signalled Tombs to follow him.

Tombs shouted something in the Irish tongue as he and Harte reluctantly walked away.

O'Connell turned to the men around the fire barrel. "How many times do they want to kill us?" he said.

The men fell silent for a long time. Then O'Connell sang a melancholic song about a boy carrying his father's sword off to war. The men stared into the flames. Delaney did too. Memories fermented in his brain like red berries in a glass jar. He saw his children's faces. Robina and Annie all smiles at his coming home. And Jimmy with his perpetual frown, wild and scheming as he ran the backyards and alleys, a mischief maker playing himself up older than he was. Holding in the tears as he sat on the boot bench in the front hall of the orphanage. No goodbye, no backwards glance to his father as MacDonald the overseer led him away.

O'Connell finished singing and looked at Delaney's shamed and saddened face. "You're seeing more in the fire than the rest of us."

"My children," Delaney said. "My son mostly, him growing into a man, and I'm not there to help him."

"Where is that?" asked the scrawny man, who still held the arm of the man with the round hat.

"Nova Scotia. I need work to get there."

"We all need work," O'Connell said.

Delaney nodded and walked from the alley. He had another hour before going to the house on Tremont Street. He walked the streets, again allowing his feet to take him wherever they wanted to go. It started snowing. He turned up the collar on his sheepskin coat and kept walking. He walked past closed shops of furniture makers and booksellers. An old man stood holding a crutch without using it. Snow gathered on the old man's shoulders.

He walked up Beacon Hill and entered a wealthy neighbour-hood of elegant two- and three-storey red brick homes, with mansard roofs and ornamental facades. The streets in this neigh-bourhood were cheerful and brightly lit with cast-iron gaslights on both sides. Outside one house a grey horse harnessed to an idle carriage stomped and steamed in the cold. Delaney rubbed its nose. The horse blinked the gathering flakes from its lashes. Delaney turned around and looked into the un-curtained window of the house where he stood.

He saw into the parlour, where dark oak woodwork framed a wallpaper garden of blue and yellow flowers. The wood was so polished the tips of the carved florets gleamed in lamplight. On the wall facing the window hung an oval, gilt-frame mirror, with twining vines as ornate as the woodwork. An attractive young woman in a heavy grey overcoat entered the parlour, stepped before the mirror, and fussed with her close-fitting fur hat. A man in a black coat and cape joined her at the mirror. Then the two turned from the mirror and came out the front door.

Delaney walked a little ways, then stepped into the shadows and waited for the man and woman to get into the carriage and drive off. He returned to the house and followed a stone walkway to a side door. He knocked three times, then gave the door three more knocks in rapid succession.

A grey-haired house servant opened the door, his black skin lacquered with lantern light. He looked hard at the visitor.

"I'm Delaney. You sent me a note."

From his green waistcoat pocket the house servant withdrew a letter and handed it to Delaney.

"I got one from Mister Colley too. He thinks highly of you."

Delaney's face emptied and his knees buckled when he read: "They strung Mister Murdock up in the barn the way those same boys had done runaways."

The house servant said, "Colley knows the ones who did it, but he's not saying. He'd be a fool to accuse white men of hanging the old man. Colley wrote that you would know who they were."

Delaney stared at him. His breathing quickened. "Murdock called them local boys with a cob up their arse."

"More than a corn cob. Hanging him like that, they knew what he had been doing before the war."

Delaney nodded. He remembered the hidey-hole in the barn, wide enough for a runaway. He looked at the letter. He read: "Billy Woods and the woman moved into the big house."

Delaney felt his face hang with grief.

"Mister Murdock knew the risk of working the underground to freedom," the house servant said. "All of us did. We expected it, almost waited for it. Never thought with the war done . . . Never thought."

Delaney folded the letter into his pocket. He fingered the sheepskin coat Murdock Murray had given him and remembered Murray smiling at him as he struggled to climb into the wagon that first time. He remembered the poultice Murray had cooked up to ease the pain in his ribs. Pressing it on and laughing at Delaney's sudden wince. Again he remembered the false wall in the horse stall and tried not to imagine the old man hanging from a beam in the barn.

"Try your luck with *Sea Flower*," the servant suggested. "It sails with the tide."

"My money played out getting here," Delaney admitted.

"Captain Nicholson's from where you're from. He sailed freedom runs before the war. You tell him Lucas Whitehead sent you. He'll be in the Seven Steps to Hell minding his crew."

Along the waterfront, every third building was a tavern. Sailors and women staggered the muddy street from one to another. Outside the Split Beam tavern, two women were scratching, biting, and punching each other. A dozen or so men cheered them on.

Delaney asked one of the men for directions to the Seven Steps to Hell. The man laughed and pointed to a red painted door not far from where they stood. Delaney ducked through the low doorway and descended seven stone steps into a windowless tavern of unplaned wood. The tavern was alive with the smell of beer, whisky, and human sweat. A loose stone fireplace and a few lanterns hanging from timber posts scattered dim pools of light around the room. A perimeter of heavy shadows favoured those patrons who wanted to go unnoticed. In the lighted centre was a long oak bar. A dozen or so men stood with their backs to it. Some watched three raggedy-dressed women flaunting themselves to the blare and tweedle of a bugle and fiddle. At one end of the bar, a few men listened to a Harvard scholar named Connor Doyle reading aloud to them for tips.

Delaney squeezed close to hear the scholar read.

"It was a very fierce storm," Doyle read. "The sea broke strange and dangerous. We hauled off upon the lanyard of the ship staff, and helped the man at the helm. We would not get down our topmast, but let all stand, because the ship scudded before the sea very well. During this storm, which was followed by a strong wind west-southwest, we were carried, by my computation, about five hundred leagues to the east, so that the oldest sailor on board could not tell in what part of the world we were."

Doyle closed the book and announced, "That was from *Gulliver's Travels* by Jonathan Swift." He tucked the book under his cloak with one hand and brought out a tin cup with the other. Some at the bar were big tippers, ringing the cup with bits and two bits.

Delaney faced the bar, embarrassed to have nothing to give. He read the large printed sign behind the bar: "On Exhibit The Accoutrements Worn By The Warriors Of Some Asiatic And African Savage Tribes." Beneath the sign was a feathered headdress.

The bartender came over, and Delaney asked if he knew Captain Nicholson. The bartender pointed to a grey-bearded man sitting with another man at a table against the far wall.

Delaney negotiated his way past several drunken men who were dancing with the three women. He approached Nicholson's table, excused himself, and begged the captain if he could have a word, adding that Lucas Whitehead had sent him. The captain gestured for Delaney to sit. He introduced the other man as Henry Croft, his first mate.

Delaney explained who he was and where he was going. The mate started to say *Sea Flower* had no need for another hand, but Captain Nicholson stopped him.

"Do you know the sea?" Nicholson asked.

"Carpenter in a shipyard most of my time and before that ship's carpenter under sail," Delaney said.

"Sailing where?"

"Coastal routes mainly. Two trips on a whaler into Hudson Bay."

Nicholson nodded to the mate, and the mate said to Delaney, "Bring your sea bag and help ready the ship. We sail on the tide."

Delaney returned to Sullivan's boarding house to fetch his belongings. On his return to the waterfront, he sensed someone following him. No one to his left or right. No one behind. Nothing but wind-blown shadows in the raw silence of that dark street. Yet he felt one of those shadows was hounding him. Maybe all of them. Dead soldiers crawling from their shallow graves. Or thieves after his empty purse. Or white men hoisting Murdock Murray to stand on nothing.

He reached into his bedroll for his carving knife. He held it along the backside of his leg. He walked with his head on a swivel. Ears pricked to the smallest of sounds.

Not far ahead a man stepped from an alley and into the light of a glassman's forge. He wore a derby hat and high-collar coat. He had something in his right hand. Held it waist high.

Delaney pressed the knife tight against his leg. He closed the distance between them.

The man held up the object in his hand. "Behold the Bridegroom passes."

Delaney saw the object in the man's hand was a Bible.

"Pray with me," the man said, lowering to his knees. "Pray for the suffering of the living. Pray for those who lie beneath."

Delaney stopped. Looked down at the man. He saw his high-collar coat had different-coloured patches and the crown had been cleanly cut from his derby.

The man raised his head. "Pray with me."

"They'd be angry prayers if I did," Delaney said. He walked away.

As he did so, the man called after him, "I will pray the door shall be open to you and you shall find what you seek."

CHAPTER 14

D elaney joined *Sea Flower's* five-man crew. They stowed what needed stowing, fixed gratings on hatchways, and nailed tarpaulins over these to keep the seawater from the stowed cargo below.

The mate ordered Delaney to assist Mrs. Roberts and her son with climbing aboard. She was the daughter of a stonemason in Boston. A pretty woman, finely dressed, dark hair combed high, side ringlets to her shoulders, brown eyes hesitant at two sailors chopping ice from the rigging.

Delaney smiled at her sudden intake of air as she felt the ship move underfoot.

The boy, in a tight-fitting frock coat and neck scarf, gripped his mother's hand. Wide-eyed with apprehension.

Delaney led them below deck to a small cabin at the stern. It was well-appointed with a bunk and hammock, a pitcher and wash basin, and two slop buckets.

Several hours later, the crew was at the capstan with their backs bent and their hands on the bars. They marched to the rhythm of the shanty man's song, round and round the drumhead as they heaved the anchor chain for a two-day sail up the Massachusetts and Maine coasts, a day to unload and load in Portland, and then a day around Grand Manan Island to Eastport, Maine. After that, Captain Nicholson said they would cross the Gulf of Maine to Nova Scotia.

Delaney loved sailing. Had it not been for marrying Mary and having three children, he would have stayed with the sea, the adventure of it. He once told her the sea was bigger than he could dream, undefined and unconnected. He had said sometimes sailing took him away from who he was, unbound by the shape of himself.

"It was time stopped and started," he had said. "A rustle of loss to give it up, Mary. That's all. A young man's life set aside for what's new for the two of us. And that old woman telling our fortune by tossing old cat bones on the ground. Remember? The Natal Day fair. What she said. It was not for us, Mary. Our future has purpose and blue skies."

She had hugged him when he had said that, as though his saying it was a statement of his love for her, his willingness to settle down, to have a family and work his trade in the shipyard. She had hugged him again when he promised her it would be forever.

Sea Flower sailed from Massachusetts Bay and no sooner skirted the shoals off Cape Ann than she ran a squall from the northeast, blowing snow and blowing up twenty-foot waves.

Nicholson was on deck, legs spread for balance, shouting orders. *Sea Flower* piled into the troughs and rose on the swells. The steersman had tied himself to the wheel, his arms bulging to hold the ship's bow to the storm. In oilskins and sou'westers, the crew shortened sail, and battened hatches and weatherboards against the sea swamping the bulwarks, sloshing the deck, and washing over the side anything not lashed down.

Delaney and Logan Sharpe, a dry-throated sailor long married to the sea, had reefed the mainsail when they saw the seasick mother and son crouched outside the fo'c'sle puking and groaning as loud as the wind. The storm and sea were having their way with them. An agony without reprieve, without escape.

Then the boy staggered to his feet and fell against the bulwark, stretching to vomit over it.

Sharpe saw the boy as drowned with the ship heeling in the blow and the crashing sea. He slipped and slid across the deck. Grabbed a scupper to stop his slide, then a handhold to regain his feet. Delaney was right behind him. They went hand over hand along the bulwark. Reaching the boy. Delaney dragging him down on the deck. Holding him there with his weight, as the ship piled off a swell and thundered through a monstrous wall of water.

Between waves, Delaney dragged the boy below deck. Sharpe had his arms around the mother. Another wave crashed. And another. Then Sharpe manoeuvred her below deck and into her cabin. He sat her beside her son against the shiplap wall. He dug hardtack from a leather pouch and gave it to the mother and boy.

"Chew it," he commanded. "Don't matter if it don't settle. You won't be choking up your insides."

Delaney and Sharpe went back to battling the storm. On captain's orders Delaney took a shift at the windlass pumping out water from below deck. Then he took his turn descending to the bottom of the hull to hold the hollow log pipe in the rising water.

The ship pitched wildly as he went below into a dark in which only what he heard and imagined seemed real. He reached the bottom of the ship's hull and stood in vile-smelling bilge water up to his knees. The hull planks squealed as though in pain. The sailor he replaced croaked his pleasure at going above.

In the light from a whale oil lantern swinging from a spike at mid-ship, Delaney grabbed the wire-wrapped log and held it in water spilling through a wide split in a plank. He saw other places where the oakum caulking had been beaten out.

Four bells on, four off, pumping bilge while the winds blew a heavy sea all that night and most of the following day. By nightfall the wind quieted and the sea calmed. Exhausted, the crew sank against the bulwarks. Despite the cold, most of them slept where they had flopped. Delaney lay on deck with his arms stretched behind his head staring at the stars. Counting them. Losing count and laughing out loud, for he was going home.

Sea Flower docked in Portland to unload barrels of grain, hogsheads of rum and molasses, and bales of cotton. With the ship unloaded, the captain sailed to a nearby beach where the crew careened *Sea Flower* for repairs. Sharpe and Delaney worked below the waterline replacing wooden planks and sealing up leaky seams. Sharpe pounded tarred rope between the wooden planks. He talked politics.

"New country," he said. "Politicians feathering for themselves, that's all it is."

"I know nothing about it," Delaney said, as he sawed a white pine board to length.

"Confederation," Sharpe said. He fit another stretch of rope into a seam and pounded it home. "Those for, those against, makes no difference. Not to me. I sail no matter who is captain."

"Don't know about it," Delaney said. He sawed a few more boards, then spiked them over the gashed planking in the hull. Sharpe roped and tarred the seams.

At Eastport, the mother and son disembarked. Both weaved and wobbled across the dock to where an old man helped them into a carriage.

Two days later, on a bright sunny winter morning, Delaney stood on deck and watched the water spray off the hull and turn to crystals in a dazzle of sunlight. Gulls circled the ship, screaming and flapping for the kitchen slops thrown over the stern.

Under full sail, *Sea Flower* caught a favourable wind and sailed into the harbour mouth. Delaney saw more than a dozen shallops, some under a single sail, others with three men at the oars, pulling for open water. Reaching from shore and out over the water were the long, wooden stages with fish shacks at the ends. He swivelled his head and saw the fish flakes along the beach. They were chockablock with salted cod.

The crew lowered sail as *Sea Flower* sailed beneath an ironstone scarp. On the scarp was a military redoubt from which a cannon fired a signal to alert the inner town of an approaching ship. *Sea Flower* sailed by a tree-covered island, McNabb's Island, with a fort and gun emplacements, and then a smaller one, George's Island, with its stone fortification around the island's perimeter.

The ship docked at Long Wharf, and Delaney disembarked. He stood on the snow-covered wharf for a moment to take in the feeling of being home. A forest of ship masts. Dray men and stevedores loading a barnyard of sheep, chickens, and pigs aboard a nearby ship. Tackling them high above the ship's bulwark in rope cribs. Chickens cackling and pigs squealing louder than the salt dry pulley blocks that lifted the load.

With his duffle in hand and bedroll across his chest, Delaney made straight for Miss Golding's Children's Refuge and Aid Home. He helloed those he met along the wooden walkway up Duke Street hill, searching their faces to see if he recognized them or they recognized him. He idled past the ornate ironwork lamp. Its base protected from rogue carriage wheels by four stone pillars in the shape of phalluses. Male passersby usually touched the pillars for luck. Delaney did the same, touching all four.

He playfully weaved his way through a work site for a three-storey stone building on Gottigen Street, around an idle derrick crane, and in and out of three-foot-by-six-foot stacks of sandstone blocks. He tight-walked a wooden plank that spanned a muck-clogged drainage ditch.

Two blocks away from the Children's Refuge and Aid Home, his pace slowed, then stopped. In a storefront window, he looked at himself. The prodigal soldier home from another country's war. A man who looked as though he had rummaged a scarecrow's closet. A red tuque that Logan Sharpe had given him. Murdock Murray's sheepskin coat. Clothes that Colley's wife had given him, grey flannel pants, shiny at the knees and frayed at the cuffs. Shaggy hair and untrimmed beard after so long on the road.

"Bedraggled," was what Mary would have called him. The Irish in her voice.

He saw her propped in the ladder-back rocker, hacking her lungs into the folds of her dress. And him holding her close, so close as to smell the stink that was rotting her from the inside out. He held her through the spasm, held her and kissed her — his lips feeling her skin like tissue paper with the flat bones of her cheeks showing through — held her so she could not see his tears, held her and with a soiled handkerchief drawn from his back pocket, wiped her lips.

He walked the two blocks to stand before the columned entrance of the Children's Refuge and Aid Home. Excitement in his eyes, half-expecting his children to run from the door and into his arms.

He doffed his red tuque and climbed the steep stairs. The building was quiet, unusually quiet for housing a host of children, no matter how disciplined or thumbed into obedience they were. He knocked without answer. Harder. Anxiety flexed into the strength of his knocks. Still no answer. He went back on the street and looked at the home.

There were no drapes, shades, or curtains on the windows. The windows on the second floor had been left open.

It seemed like ages ago when he had stood outside this building, overwhelmed by its size. He now tried to see into the front room that was Miss Golding's office. The upward angle from the street hemmed his view of the room to little more than a small portion of the ceiling and crown moulding on the far wall.

A longing nudged him forward. Again he climbed the stairs. This time he tried the door. The lock turned, but the door was swollen tight. He shouldered it open and entered, closing the door behind. He stood in the dark shadows of the oak-panelled front hall, standing in the same spot where he had stood six years ago outside Miss Golding's office. Hat in hand. Stooped by the weight of his decision.

The office was completely empty. Not a scrap of paper had been left behind. Sunlight spilled over the floor, which the yellow and blue carpet had covered. It pooled where the rosewood side table with the carved lion's head had stood. The painting of the apple pickers was gone; the wall was shadowed where the painting had hung.

He dropped his duffle and cap and lost his breath in a gasp that sounded to the pit of his stomach. He gulped air and gulped more, then let it out in a blast of astonishment.

He felt as though the room had been waiting for him, waiting with its torment, waiting to accuse him of signing away his children into her care. He heard the emptiness of that empty space. He felt that emptiness in his heart. He sunk to his haunches, pained to remember when he had gone home after signing that agreement with Miss Golding.

He had tried chasing his children around the kitchen the way he had always done, expecting them to erupt into peals of laughter. Only Annie ran from his chase. Jimmy and Robina refused to budge, standing their ground when he ran for them.

They let him tickle their sides without laughing. They waited for him to tell them what he tried to hide behind his foolishness and larky smile.

The details came out slowly during supper that night. A refuge and aid home. But not for long. Be home before they know it. Obligated to go if he believed in abolition. Not saying that his joining up was an honourable excuse for running away from the fear of raising them without their mother.

Jimmy had slurped his soup to keep from crying, and Robina had retreated to that faraway place in her head where only Annie could go to find her.

Delaney now turned from Miss Golding's office and walked through the dark hall where he had allowed MacDonald the Overseer to lead his children away from him. He passed through the empty parlour, his scuffed boots hollow-sounding against the high ceiling of plastered tin. He turned down a narrow hall and into the scullery.

Light from two large windows filled the room. The windows overlooked the carriage house. There was a black iron cook-stove and a long harvest table. Delaney opened the saltbox. It was empty. So was the flour bin. A ratty cloth hung from a hook nailed into the chair rail, which ran along the top of pine wainscotting. Beside the cloth was a hand pump and a white enamel sink. The sink was half-filled with scummy water. A greasy cloth plugged the drain. Delaney reached into the sink and removed the cloth plug. He watched the water drain.

He stood there staring at the drain for a long time after the water was gone. From upstairs, he heard footsteps. He went into the hall. At the foot of the hall stairs, he heard whispering. He climbed the stairs. The whispering stopped. On the second floor landing he smelled what he thought was the odour of charred wood. The second floor was where the girls had slept. He remembered the night before he had left for the war, standing on the sidewalk in the dark and watching silhouettes pass behind the curtained glass. He had wondered if one of the taller ones was Robina, and whether Annie was with her.

Now he entered a room at the front of the house. It was empty. Snow had blown through an open window and across the room and piled against the opposite wall. He closed the window. He crossed the hall and entered another room. It too was empty. The window in this room was also open, and snow had blown in. As he closed the window, he saw girls' names scratched into the window jamb and sill. He looked for Robina and Annie's names. They were not there.

He went back to the first room and to the window. He saw more girls' names scratched into the woodwork. On the sill, scratched tight together, as though they were one name, he read "RobinaAnnie."

He fingered the names. Feeling for the hands that had scratched them. Seeing their faces in the window glass. Hearing them squeal with delight the time he had taken them to the shipyard to show them the figurehead another man had carved. Annie had wanted to touch the carved woman with golden hair and a deep blue dress. Robina had simply hung on his arm, gripping it, content to look at the beautiful woman who would be mounted to the bow of a clipper ship.

Again he heard whispering. It came from one of the rooms at the back of the house. As he walked the long, dark hallway, the smell of charred wood became more pronounced. The door was closed on the room to his left. He opened it to see a frightened old man huddled in the corner. An old woman shielded him, her fists clenched and her back up.

At the centre of the room was a makeshift firebox. It had been fashioned from a tin scrap and rudely bent to a rectangular shape. Inside it were charred boards. Delaney saw where the couple had pried baseboards from the wall. By the wood chips at his feet, he guessed they had leaned the boards against the door frame and broken them with their weight.

He held open his arms to them, as though offering himself in peace. The man covered his face and shrunk into himself. The woman poked out her chin and balled her fists.

Delaney spoke softly. "Where are the children?"

The old man curled deeper into the corner. The feisty woman leaned forward and said, "Gone."

"Gone where?"

Again the old man cowered.

"To a farm," the old woman said.

"A farm?"

"I don't know where," she said. "It could be anywhere."

Delaney walked. He wrung out failure with each step. No helloes to those he passed. No recognition as to where he was. Before long he reached Point Pleasant, a forested park where he had often picnicked with Mary and their children. He walked a snowy path through dense woods. He did so without knowing he was walking it. At the Martello Tower, a squat round fort, he stopped and pressed his head against the ironstone masonry. His heart hurt into his face.

He turned from the tower and started down another snowy path. It skirted a ridge that fell off to a saltwater inlet. The path swung into denser forest, then opened to a glade with a large beech tree at the centre of it. The initial tree, he and Mary had called it. He searched for where he had carved their initials on the side facing away from the path, where he had spread his coat on the ground that soft summer night, and they had fumbled off each other's clothes and had loved each other for the first time, where he had promised marriage on what each had given and the other had shared.

He slumped against the tree, closed his eyes, and covered his face with his hands. He saw his frightened children as they reluctantly followed the Overseer from that dark hallway in the Children's Refuge and Aid Home and were shut from his life with the closing of a door. He huddled against his duffle and curled into his sheepskin coat. He shivered himself to sleep.

❦

He woke still shivering and from the grief heaving in his empty stomach. He pulled himself to his feet and looked at the carved letters in the tree. He heard the wind in the branches, and the birds. He heard his voice, or maybe it was Mary's, clean sounding in the icy air, words taking shape in the winter light, saying over and over that he must get the children back, he must get them back, he must.

The ground seemed to break underfoot. He lost his balance over loose cobbles and caught it before falling.

"They're not *her* children," he said out loud.

He was near the food office for the poor, and mothers who had already begun to queue for morning bread heard him and looked.

"They're mine, mine and Mary's," he said even louder, defiantly poking out his chin at the mothers as though they were responsible for his shame. He tightened his grip on his duffel and continued walking, slower. His feet now felt the doubt that had been piling up in his mind.

He pulled up short in front of St. Paul's Church and stared blankly at the gutter water pooling in the cracked cobblestone at his feet. A white-haired priest in a black cassock opened the church door for morning service and nodded to him. Delaney heard a wagon rumble past, and the driver calling "Good morning" to a shopkeeper who was throwing open the shutters on his leather goods store. He heard young men hollering to each other outside Dalhousie College.

The priest walked from the church and across Dalhousie Square to Delaney. They looked into each other's eyes.

"You look troubled," the priest said.

Delaney nodded.

CHAPTER 15

A s she did most nights, Robina tossed and turned on her narrow bed beside the kitchen stove, afraid to sleep for the prison dreams she had. She got up and lit a taper from the stove and then an iron frame lamp. She pulled on a woollen coat and left the log house to walk from the French settlement. The settlement consisted of three houses, a cow, sheep and horse barn, a chicken coop, and a shed. She followed the upper path through the woods to where she sat on a flat rock on a hilltop overlooking a small stream.

After blowing out the lamp and folding her hands in her lap to quiet them from scratching her arms and face, she hummed a song her mother sang. A lullaby that exposed her heart to worry and confusion. Worry for her sister lost in the shuffle of time. Confused after her two years among the rats and roaches in a damp cell in the Saint John prison. Two years because Sheriff Greene had spoken to the court on her behalf. Released to wander. Defensive. Trusting no one. Until these French families saw her sleeping on the side of a road.

Madame LeBlanc was the matriarch. Her two sons and their wives and children worked the farm and woodlot together. She spoke only French, and Robina spoke only English, yet both knew what each other meant without knowing what each other said. There was laughter like Robina hadn't heard in years. Children squealing with happiness. Shared meals.

Madame LeBlanc loved her family, in the same way Robina remembered her mother having loved hers, cherishing her children through her pain. Praying a dying promise from their father to keep them all together, and from Robina to look after Annie.

Robina heard the squeak and rattle of the wagon long before she saw it stop on the side of the dirt road near the stream. Five men got out. Three lit cattail torches soaked in animal fat. The men without torches carried rifles. They travelled the path along the stream, single file, past where Robina was sitting unseen. Taking their time. Careful.

She lost sight of them where the path swung away from the stream and into the woods. She could still hear the crunch of their leather boots in the dry autumn leaves. Another wagon rumbled on the road and stopped behind the first. It was a deep-bellied farm wagon, the kind used for hauling manure to the fields. Except for the driver, the farm wagon was empty.

Robina got up and slowly followed the upper path back toward the settlement. She ducked behind a spruce thicket and watched the gang of men enter a clearing in which a pile of logs had been yarded for squaring into timber.

One of the men gathered the others around him, whispering. He removed a coil of rope from his shoulder. Another man pulled a knife and cut several three-foot lengths from the coil. He hung the lengths around his neck, and handed the remainder of the coil back to the leader.

Robina crouched lower behind the spruce bushes and watched the men pull from their pants pockets flour bags with the eyes cut out. They covered their heads and marched to the settlement.

Robina crept forward through the undergrowth. Her face drawn in fear to see the men with rifles take a stand at the centre of the settlement. Two of the men with torches stood at two of the houses. The leader then tossed his torch into the barn. The two with torches lit the houses on fire. The man nearest the third house, Madame LeBlanc's house, torched that one.

The cow, horse, and three sheep clamoured wildly to get out. The LeBlanc men, women, and children, all in nightshirts, ran screaming from their burning houses. Madame LeBlanc and one of the women carried infants. The other woman had three toddlers in tow. All were wide-eyed at the blaze, panicky, flapping their arms, turning every which way; not knowing what to do or where to go.

Then the riflemen fired above their heads.

The French families stopped suddenly. Each of them gasped as though the Earth had run out of air. They saw the hooded men and huddled together.

The riflemen trained their rifles on them. Two of the hooded men dropped their torches and tied the hands of the French men and women and roped their waists so they could be led away like prisoners. As one of the hooded men tied her hands, Madame LeBlanc cried out Robina's name and said something in French.

Robina watched from behind the spruce thicket, holding her breath, shaking uncontrollably.

The hooded men led the French families back the way they had come. Robina returned to the flat rock by the upper path and watched the families being loaded into the farm wagon. Madame LeBlanc, still carrying an infant, was the last to get in.

After the farm wagon had driven off, the men removed their hoods. They were talking loud and laughing. In the torchlight, Robina recognized one of them from the hardware store in Woodstock. She heard this man say, "Run them French bastards out."

Another man said, "See if the goddamn Indians want them."

Robina carefully returned along the path and sat at the edge of the settlement. The stink of burned animal flesh filled the air. She remained there long after the buildings had burned to the ground. She stared at the smouldering ruins. The challenge of what had been was now gone. Hope as dead as the ashes.

Robina understood what Madame LeBlanc had cried out. "Cave de racine." She went to the root cellar, which had been dug into the side of a hill. She opened the heavy plank door. She propped the door open with a stick. The inside walls were lined with stone. The wooden racks were filled with vegetables fresh from the harvest: carrots, turnip, beets, onions, cabbage, and squash. There was a barrel of apples, another of potatoes covered with sand. There was a barrel half-filled with pickled pork. A slaughtered calf hung from a beam, waiting to be butchered, salted, and stored.

Robina ate an apple, then closed the root cellar door and went poking among the smoking ruins. She found a copper kettle and a wooden bowl and Madame LeBlanc's twig-work rocker, which miraculously had not been touched by the fire.

The hooded men had not set the shed on fire. Inside were farming tools: scythes, hay rakes, shovels, hoes, saws, axes. Robina cleared out enough to make room for the rocker. She sat in it and went to sleep.

She slept long into the night and woke to a darkness that was joyless. She left the shed and stood in what little light spread from a horned moon. She smelled the charred ruins and burnt animal flesh.

At first light, she returned to the shed and found a wicker apple-picker's basket. In the root cellar, she filled the basket with whatever she could eat without cooking: apples, potatoes, carrots, beets, and onions. She slipped the basket over her head and tied the bottom ropes around her waist. Once more she poked through the ruins. This time she found a knife with a bone handle.

She walked the path along the stream to the road and stood there for a time, unsure which direction to take. At last, she decided to turn left and follow the road as far as it would take her. She walked for hours. Her feet hurt in the wooden shoes she wore. At a crossroads, she curled under a tall pine and ate a carrot and a potato. She fell asleep. Again she woke in the middle of the night. The darkness was impenetrable. The silence frightened her. She knew if she cried out no one would hear, not even the angels her mother had told her about, not even God.

CHAPTER 16

W aves riffled on the cobble beach and lapped at
the pilings of the fish shack at the end of the
stage. Inside the shack, the plank floor and walls
smelled of old fish guts and dried blood. Jimmy slept in the loft
on a stack of canvas sail. The stage was built of spruce poles and
cross braces, with rafters running the length of it. Ship canvas
covered the far end that jutted eighty to a hundred feet over
the water.

He woke to the gulls screaming and the pipers crying and to
voices carrying on the water through the sea fog. He climbed
down and walked from the shack and along the beach to where
two men were removing a pile of salted fish that was already
cured. They restacked the pile onto barrows.

"A clean day," one of them said, pointing to the sun burning
through the fog.

Jimmy helped them push the load to the washing site where the salted fish would be submerged and washed, drained, then hung to dry on raised wooden frames called flakes.

The squinty-eyed one talked about Ryan the cobbler's daughter. He called her "loose mutton" or "a ewe in rags," and how she did the things men only dream of doing with their wives.

Jimmy laughed without really knowing what he was laughing at.

The same man pointed to a shallop drawing alongside the stage.

Jimmy ran to where the boat was docking, grabbed a gaff on the way, and boarded the shallop. He joined thirteen-year-old Jeremy Blanchard at gaffing cod from the fishing boat, and flinging them over their heads onto the deck of the canvas-roofed stage. Two other boys loaded the fish into tubs and lugged the tubs to the twenty-foot-long splitting table. Before long, there was a steady supply of fish from a dozen or so shallops, which plied the fishing grounds within a league or two from the mouth of the harbour.

As he gaffed a fish and flung it, Jimmy saw the admiral march to the end of the stage. The admiral was a tall, solidly built man, with pinched shoulders and a composure as tight as a long length of braided rope. His mouth twisted into a perpetual scowl from the way his left cheekbone caved inward. He was the man in charge, the stand-in for the bosses who ran the operation from an office in Halifax and another in Boston. The admiral ordered Jimmy to join a second crew at dressing the fish.

For the rest of the day, Jimmy stood up to his knees inside a low wooden barrel at the splitting table. The fringe of his long leather apron hung outside the tub so fish waste would not run into it. His mittened hands were awkward with the knife, as he sliced open a cod's throat and flashed up its belly. He was "the throater" in a three-man splitting crew.

"The header," a sandy-haired youth, pulled off the head and removed the guts, dropping the waste through a hole in the staging to the water below, careful with the liver and roe, which he placed into separate buckets.

"The splitter," a dark-skinned, hard-bitten man, was the handy one with a knife. He removed the backbone with one clean cut, leaving the surrounding flesh firm and undamaged.

They dressed a steady supply of fish, and worked into the evening by torchlight. The admiral came by with two hurricane lamps. He told the dressing crews that one shallop had not returned from the fishing grounds.

"Who is it?" someone asked.

"Reardon," the admiral said.

The splitter in Jimmy's crew volunteered both himself and Jimmy to wait for Reardon's boat. As the others walked off, Jimmy and the splitter lashed the hurricane lamps to tall poles so the incoming boat could see the light from the mouth of the harbour. They used barrows to brace the poles against bollards at the head of the stage.

They sat on the splitting table to wait, silent for the longest time, looking out to sea for the bow light on the shallop. Then the splitter mumbled something about the sea at night and the men out there living between two graves.

Jimmy said he didn't understand.

The splitter's eye sockets were dark in the overhead lamplight, his voice dreary and inconsolable. "One grave the others dig for us, and one we dig for ourselves."

He raised his right leg and drew a knife from his boot. "I work the splitting table," he said, taking a stone from a pocket and honing the blade. "Walk away whenever I want." He pointed the knife toward the harbour mouth. "They fish for the price the admiral sets. Overfilling their boats. Starving or drowning. They can't walk away from what their fathers done. They can't walk away from nothing."

Jimmy looked to where the splitter was pointing and saw sea fog rolling into the harbour on a southeast wind. The fog bell on Devil's Island gonged. So did the one at Chebucto Head. Both of them deep and mournful.

"Thick fog," the splitter said. "A goddamn blindfold on the old man and Carson his son. A menace running their luck like that."

Jimmy strained to see against the strength of the night and strained more to see through the bank of fog.

The splitter pulled a tobacco plug from his coat pocket and cut off a chew. He offered to cut one for Jimmy.

Jimmy shook his head. His eyes skinned through a layer of fog and stabbed at the dark to see a dim light rising and falling. He yelped and jumped off the table and ran to the head of the stage. He waved his arms and hollered.

The splitter put away the knife and stone and came beside him.

"No burning fish bones with them," he said. "Being blessed or being lucky don't matter now."

The shallop broke ahead of the fog bank, and when Jimmy saw its main sail and jib, he rose with jubilation. He hooted and hollered.

Old Man Reardon lowered sail, then grabbed the oar and drew the boat alongside the stage. There was no sign of Carson on board. The old man threw lines to the splitter and to Jimmy, and they tied them off to bollards.

Jimmy climbed down to help unload the catch. In the glow from the lantern at the bow, Jimmy saw twenty-year-old Carson sitting toward the stern, with fish at his feet. His wide body hulked over his knees. He was holding his face in his hands. Jimmy started gaffing fish to the stage.

"We netted her," Reardon was saying to the splitter. "In the water a while. Come out on a tide and caught a current, I should think."

Jimmy worked his way toward the stern, working up a sweat despite the damp chill from the fog. He reached Carson and said, "You got to move."

The young man lifted his head, his face in rags. He held out his hands in a helpless gesture. Then he leaned forward and cleared fish away from his feet. He began to cry.

Jimmy looked down at the pile of fish. In the dim light he saw the bloated face of a woman. Her long brown hair snarled in the fish net and one of her eyes eaten out. Jimmy gagged and turned away. He reeled and staggered and grabbed a gunwale for support.

"The dead pester my boy something awful," Reardon said to the splitter, pointing at his son. He pointed at Jimmy. "Him too, it looks. Death takes getting used to, but it's hard seeing too much of it."

The splitter boarded the boat and squeezed past Jimmy and Reardon's son and looked at the body. "Can't tell how old she is," he said.

"A woman," Reardon said. "Or an older girl by the length of her."

The splitter ordered Jimmy to the stage and climbed up after him. He rigged a block and tackle, and the two of them hoisted the body.

Reardon gaffed fish to the stage. "I fished alone after we caught her."

Jimmy, still squeamish to look at the dead woman, fetched a canvas scrap from the sail loft. The splitter rolled the body into it.

"It's the admiral's now," he said. He drew his knife from his boot and stood at the splitting table. "Dress this catch and we'll go for a jar."

Jimmy stood beside the sail-wrapped body, staring at it. Tearing up. His voice faltering. "I got sisters."

The splitter flapped three fish on the splitting table.

"And they got me," Jimmy said. "I'm all they got." He flung open his arms, as though flinging away emptiness.

The splitter grabbed a fish and in three quick strokes gutted it, beheaded it, and cut out the backbone. He stabbed the knife into the splitting table. Without facing Jimmy he said, "It's a dead woman. That's all it is. She drowned or drowned herself." He looked at Jimmy. "It means nothing to us. But if you want to walk, then go walk."

"I got sisters," Jimmy insisted.

The splitter grabbed his knife and reached for another fish. He gutted it and sliced off the head. He changed his grip on the knife and angrily stabbed it through the fish and into the splitting table. He hung his head for a moment, then lifted it and turned to see Jimmy halfway to the fish shack.

The splitter hollered after him, "Hug the shadows if you know what's good for you. Don't never show yourself. Goddamn it, boy, don't never."

CHAPTER 17

A nnie pumped water from a pump behind the white, rambling house. The pump whooped and gurgled and gushed to fill her wooden bucket. It was a heavy load for a girl her size. "Frail," was how Dr. Putnam summed up her medical examination. "Starved," was how Mrs. Williamson described her to her husband when she brought Annie home from New Brunswick more than a year ago. "I don't know how those Clooneys could've treated her like that, working her to skin and bones. A court order be darned."

Mrs. Williamson met Annie at the well.

"How many times, Miss Annie Delaney?" she scolded, smiling as she said it. "I have two boys to carry heavy loads."

"Two lazy boys," Annie shot back, her tone matching Mrs. Williamson's, her smile every bit as broad. "And they're not here anyway."

Together they carried the bucket into the kitchen and set it beside the long copper sink.

Annie folded a linen cloth and laid it on top of a basket made of interwoven strips of black ash.

Mrs. Williamson scooped water from the bucket and poured it over a colander of fresh-picked blueberries.

"We'll see how lazy my boys are working the oats for Mr. Duggan," she said.

"No tolerance on his part," Annie said.

"He's not like their father," Mrs. Williamson said.

"I doubt Mister Williamson ever worked anyone hard," Annie said, defending the man who had paid for her ticket to travel by train from New Brunswick to Smiths Falls, Ontario. The man who could not help smiling happily whenever she entered a room.

"Clerking a dry goods store is not exactly hard work," Mrs. Williamson said. She removed the berries to a bowl, which she covered with a tight-fitting square of beeswaxed linen. "It's his knees giving way to the up and down of it. And you know what those boys said about not wanting a life in dry goods. Their father thinks fieldwork might help them change their minds."

They loaded the basket and water bucket into a buggy pulled by a brown mare.

"You know how it is," Mrs. Williamson said. "You had a brother."

Annie saddened. She missed Jimmy as much as she missed Robina. Her mind elbowing out the sharp-edged memories of her mother dying and her father kissing her goodbye, of loneliness with the Clooneys and Robina inside a jail cell. Instead she clung to remembering chasing Jimmy and Robina around stacks of tarred oak beams at the shipyard. Walking from the slips with their father. "Last one home is a rotten egg." Running as fast as she could to catch up. And Jimmy turning back and screaming for her to "stop." His face wildly distorted. And her stopping short of running under horse hooves and wagon wheels.

"I don't know what I want for those boys." Mrs. Williamson clicked her tongue on her teeth and flicked the reins. "And I don't know what I want for you, Miss Annie Delaney. A husband likely, though they come with a burden, and don't I know it."

They travelled less than two miles on a dusty road to a battle-field of stubble. Under a maple with low-hanging branches, they spread the linen cloth. An extravagance for men with their faces covered in oat hulls from working the thresher. Annie cut slices of bread and buttered them. Mrs. Williamson set out the berries and the carved ham. She called to the men. Her voice deadened by the draft horse walking the wide belt on the thresher, which gulped like a pond full of frogs. She walked toward them. Crunched through the stubble. One of the boys looked up and saw her. He signalled Duggan, and Duggan stopped the horse's steady pace.

The boys and Duggan walked over. Duggan nodded at the spread of food on the cloth. He winked to the boys.

"Annie's learning the ways of a woman," he said. "You tell your older friends be careful."

After supper, Annie and Mrs. Williamson walked arm in arm along the main street through Smiths Falls. Mr. Williamson and the boys reluctantly followed. A promenade, Mrs. Williamson called it. An evening ritual to assist the digestion. An easy way to share one's thoughts and opinions.

"I'll warn you before we return home," Mrs. Williamson said. "He'd like you to work the store with him. You're old enough and smarter than either one of my boys. You're good with people. He noticed."

"I'd like that," Annie said.

"I insisted he pay wages."

Annie raised her hands in protest.

"He pays the boys whenever they work," Mrs. Williamson said. "It's only fair."

CHAPTER 18

Arthur Delaney had worked three months on the Dartmouth Slips to hire William Drysdale, a lawyer. Now they stepped from the stagecoach outside the feed and grain store in Aylesford.

A big man with a V-shaped body and heavy eyebrows, which defined his square, tough-to-the-world face, introduced himself as Sheriff Fletcher. His handshake matched his face. Delaney gave The Toughness right back. With Drysdale, the Sheriff eased off, as though respecting the lawyer's sickly complexion and unusually thin frame.

Sheriff Fletcher led them to two carriages waiting nearby. The lead carriage was empty. A woman sat in the front seat of the second carriage. A gangly man in a frock coat and choker collar stood beside it. Sheriff Fletcher introduced the man as Reverend Ezra Morton of St. Boniface Anglican Church, and the woman as the reverend's wife, Eleanor.

Reverend Morton had a jovial smile that never seemed to stop. He didn't so much shake Delaney's hand as pray it between both of his. He did the same to Drysdale.

"You must understand we had no way of knowing about Miss Golding's past," Reverend Morton confided, still smiling, though his voice, much deeper than what he looked, had taken on a serious tone. "There have been accusations. Inquiries. Nothing proven, not yet. But we . . . You see, she called Hillside Farm a New Jerusalem for orphans. It was so promising."

Reverend Morton looked to Sheriff Fletcher for confirmation of this, but Sheriff Fletcher had already walked to the lead carriage and climbed in to take the reins. Drysdale got in beside him.

Eleanor Morton wore a grey bonnet and grey dress. The bonnet and dress matched the cold shoulder she gave Delaney as he climbed into the seat behind her.

"It has been a while since you saw them last," Reverend Morton said to Delaney, flicking the reins to get going, then steering the horse and carriage around a mudhole in the road. "We read the court documents."

Eleanor sat with her hands flat on the grey wool blanket on her lap. "Not too close," she warned her husband.

Reverend Morton backed off from the lead carriage, holding far enough behind to avoid the clots and spray thrown up from the soggy road.

"Near seven years," Delancy answered. He leaned forward in the back seat and a lock of dark hair fell across his forehead. "My wife died and I . . . I worry they won't remember."

Eleanor Morton set her jaw in a look that was all business. "Other than your wife being dead, there was another reason you gave up your children?"

"There was," Delaney admitted. His voice contrite. "There was."

"It was not your affair to join that war," she said.

Reverend Morton hastened to add, his voice less pointed than his wife's. "According to Miss Golding's affidavit, she believed you were killed in a battle. She told the children that. Eleanor will explain it to them."

Delaney nodded and sank into the leather cushion. The clopping of the horses on the road and the rumble of the carriages filled the silence. He released his mind to follow his eyes through the passing trees, to where a memory crept from the underwood, gaining shape the more he stared at it — Miss Emma Golding sitting at her walnut desk and opening a drawer for pen, ink, and blotting paper, then dipping the pen and positioning a document for Delaney to sign. He remembered her rosewater smell. His hand trembled his name in tiny letters on the bottom of the page.

He blinked the memory from his eyes and turned his attention to the country road bending right at Dempsey's Corner. It was lined with maples whose crowns had leaned over the road to form a long archway of branches. The carriages clattered on the plank bridge across Graves Brook. To the left, beyond a wire fence, was a sawmill with the mill wheel turning. To the right, on the near side of a spinney of blue spruce, there ran a long field over which a deep wagon rumbled. From the wagon, boys shovelled manure.

Delaney searched the boys' faces for Jimmy. He thought he saw him and leaned from the carriage for a better look. The road swung closer to the field and close to where the wagon rumbled. Delaney stood and waved. The boys waved back. The boy he had taken for Jimmy lifted his head and called something to the passing carriages. The boy hardly resembled Jimmy at all.

Delaney leaned back, crossed his legs. He uncrossed them. His fingers tapped his knees. He scanned the long field and orchard of apple blossoms. He crossed his legs again, and uncrossed them. He took a deep breath, and inched forward, leaning to favour Eleanor Morton.

"I never stopped loving them for a single moment. What I saw, the bodies I buried . . . The years of regret. I don't need your scolding."

The carriages splashed through a stream of runoff from North Mountain. The water creamed around the wheels. Reverend Morton pointed to the large white house surrounded by maples. He announced: "Hillside Farm."

Eleanor swung and faced Delaney. Her expression was forgiving. "You will be surprised what children remember. And the youngest will remember the most."

When the carriages rolled into the farmyard, an old man and three boys were mucking the barn and stable. Two girls were sorting seeds and sets. All of them stopped what they were doing to see who had come.

Delaney searched their faces for Jimmy, Robina, and Annie. They were not among them.

Drysdale fumbled papers from a wooden case he had carried on his lap and handed them to Sheriff Fletcher. He then climbed from the carriage and walked back to help Eleanor to the ground. He stopped Delaney from getting out. "Remember what we discussed."

Delaney stared blankly.

"Remain in the carriage," Drysdale insisted. "Sheriff Fletcher will execute the court order, and I will speak on your behalf. When the children are delivered, Mrs. Morton and Reverend Morton will bring them to you. Please. Miss Golding knows why we are here."

Delaney watched Drysdale and the delegation step onto the wraparound porch and through the front door. Not far from where he stood a well pump coughed. A bucket clattered. He turned and saw a girl who was twelve, perhaps thirteen, drawing a bucket of water and carrying it into the summer kitchen. She passed two younger girls who were beating dust from a large brown carpet folded over a rope line that ran from the back stoop to a stately maple. The afternoon sun filtered through the branches of the maple and draped the girls in a weave of thin shadows and sunlight.

He watched the two girls for a moment, then, despite Drysdale's instructions, climbed from the carriage. He wanted to be ready when his children ran from the house and into his arms. He wanted the reunion to happen as he had imagined it happening, all of them rushing to one another and saying what for years had been trapped in their hearts.

One of the girls, the one in a blue smock with a grey apron, sensed him looking and stopped beating. She stepped away from the carpet and along the back stoop. "Who are you?" She asked when she was near enough for Delaney to hear without her having to raise her voice.

"Arthur Delaney. I'm Robina, Jimmy, and Annie's father. Do you know them?"

The girl nodded and brushed a strand of light brown hair from her face. Delaney could now see that the girl had freckles and skin tanned from the outdoor work.

"Robina and me were friends a while back," she said. "She taught me sewing." The girl turned to go back to beating the carpet.

It tickled Delaney to hear this. "And Annie, are you friends with Annie?"

The girl faced him and nodded. She looked at the house and then again at Delaney. "They went away a long time ago."

Just then the front door opened and Drysdale emerged waving a page of foolscap in his hand.

What the girl had said puzzled Delaney. What puzzled him more was the disappointment that hung from Drysdale's face.

"They're not here," Drysdale said, striding down the gravel path. He held out the page of foolscap as though that explained it.

"No," Delaney replied, still puzzled, mistaking Drysdale's statement for a question. "They must be inside."

Drysdale shook his head, and his thin body shook with it. "No, Arthur, they're not!"

"Then they're . . ." What Drysdale was saying and what the young girl had said suddenly struck him. Delaney swung to the girls in the storage shed. He searched their faces. One girl carried a wicker basket from the shed and set it in the back of a wagon. She looked at Delaney and looked away.

His tongue moved, but no words came from his mouth. He noticed that the girl had a hole in the side of her brown smock and that the hem was soiled with mud. He noticed too that a shed door was broken where it scraped over the ground. He saw a hammer lying on a wooden bench outside the shed. Beside it was a cracked stone jug full of cobwebs. He felt his stomach tighten. He closed his eyes and saw Robina and Jimmy the way he had seen them last on the boot bench in the dark hallway in the Children's Refuge and Aid Home, unsmiling; Robina deep inside her personal envelope of silence, and Jimmy sitting on his hands and not budging out of spite. He saw Annie the way he always remembered her, lacing her fingers behind his head and wishing him "Good morning."

"Arthur!" Drysdale called and followed his own voice to where Delaney had crouched in the farmyard. The lawyer's soft leather shoes sank in the mud. "She indentured them. Jimmy more than two years ago, the girls not long after." Again Drysdale held up the page of foolscap to show that it was all written down.

Delaney refused to look at the written page. He faced the house and the girls beating the carpet, then snapped his head toward the boys and old man who were mucking the stable.

He stumbled toward the stable and called for his son through the open door. His voice banged off the heavy beams and board walls. The old man and boys straightened at the sound of it. The boys cowered at the sight of Delaney standing in the double door with his face on fire, challenging the tallest of the boys to tell him where his son was working. "Jimmy Delaney, where is he?"

The old man in muck-stained trousers held up by rope braces limped from a stall. He said to Delaney. "She sold Jimmy back a time."

"Sold him?"

The old man's face puckered, swelling out the liver stains on his skin. He looked sadly at Delaney. "Others too."

Drysdale hurried across the farmyard to join Delaney at the stable door. "She indentured Jimmy to Rufus DeWolfe," Drysdale said.

"Sold him," the old man quickly added. "But he run away."

Drysdale held up the written page as though to confirm what the old man had said.

"Jimmy worked with me in the mill. My name's Horsnell. We were friends."

Delaney shook all over. His head swivelled from Horsnell and the boys in the stable to the big house, and to the orchard and the tree-covered hillside, where three boys pushed a cart up a rocky path and into the woods.

"They're not here," Drysdale emphasized. "Look! This is what she provided, a detective's report on their last-known whereabouts."

"Last?"

Drysdale lowered his voice to calm his client. "Those who bought the girls' indentures later sold them to someone else. Traded them. No records were kept."

The front door opened, and Reverend Morton and Eleanor emerged from the house. Sheriff Fletcher was close behind, angrily shaking his head at something Reverend Morton had said.

"They're here!" Delaney insisted. He broke from Drysdale and charged for the wraparound porch and the front door.

Sheriff Fletcher caught him on the stone path and struggled to hold him from entering the house. Delaney lost his footing on the uneven ground. He stumbled and fell to one knee. Sheriff Fletcher held him down.

"Go in there and you're trespassing," Sheriff Fletcher ordered. "She'll lay charges."

The two men locked eyes, both breathing fast to feed the pace of their hearts.

Eleanor Morton reached past Sheriff Fletcher to touch Delaney's shoulder.

He raised a hand to hers. His words were dry and cracked, like an empty barrel left in the sun. "What's happened? What went wrong?"

Eleanor shook her head. Her eyes filled. "I don't know what to answer."

Delaney looked past Eleanor and Sheriff Fletcher, and past Reverend Morton who was still standing on the wraparound porch. His eyes settled on Emma Golding in the front window, watching him. Behind the glare in the glass, her face was winter.

❧

It was not until they were on the stagecoach to Windsor that Drysdale handed Delaney the page of foolscap. It bore the name and address of the detective agency: *Brown and Quinn, 47 Pleasant Street, Halifax*. Delaney read the report.

> *Jimmy Delaney placed with Rufus DeWolfe of Stewiacke, Nova Scotia. Stayed two years and ran away. No known whereabouts to date.*

Annie Delaney placed with John Tuttle of Pugwash,
Nova Scotia. Bond sold to persons unknown. No known
whereabouts to date.

Robina Delaney placed with John Tuttle of Pugwash,
Nova Scotia. Bond sold to persons unknown. No known
whereabouts to date.

Delaney reread the document several times. He tried to imagine his children crowded together with their mother on the daybed, laughing and singing some foolish song from when she had been a little girl.

"I know Delong Brown," Drysdale suggested. "He may know more than what he wrote in that report."

Drysdale looked off Delaney to the passing countryside. He continued: "She invited us for tea. Offered the Mortons a tour of the main house and the boys' dormitory. Suggested Fletcher and I might want to inspect the stable and barns. Then she handed me that. She said her lawyer assured her that it complies with the court order. She claimed it proves she did what she could to find them."

Delaney folded the paper and stuffed it into his coat pocket.

The coach slowed and stopped at Cambridge Station to change horses, and to give Drysdale and Delaney a chance to stretch their legs. The stage stop was a long wood-frame building sheathed in clapboard and painted red.

Drysdale went to the outhouse. Delaney walked the road in the direction from which they had come. The road took a turn and soon he was out of sight.

He followed the road past apple orchards with branches budding, and over flat, ploughed farmland that exhaled the earthy smell of spring. He passed a farmyard where hundreds of empty wooden apple barrels were stacked in neat rows beneath an open-air shed with a tin roof. Three apple barrels stood like bow-bellied soldiers guarding a wagon path that crossed over the road. He walked toward sunset. He walked with purpose.

It was sundown when he reached Aylesford. Up ahead, the station glowed with the dull, yellow light of kerosene lamps and lanterns. Delaney abandoned the tracks so as not to be seen by those smoking and talking outside the station. He struck off through the town of squat wood-frame houses for the bumpy road to Dempsey's Corner.

A cold wind blew through the valley, but not cold enough to cool down the fire of feelings that stoked his legs to charge double-time on that dirt road. In his eyes were his children's faces lost somewhere on a country road like this, or staring at a wooden ceiling from a hard wooden bunk and damning their father for having given them away. And there was her face too, Miss Golding's, in the big front window at Hillside Farm, mocking the hopelessness of his effort to get his children back. His feet pounded harder. His eyes tightened their grip on the dark shadows across the road. He kicked at the dirt, punched at the wind, and held down a cry that would have unleashed the anger that was coiled inside.

He had no thought for what he meant to do when he got to Hillside Farm, just a churning inside to face her down and make her knuckle in front of him, to shout that smile from her face, the smile that he kept seeing no matter which way he looked. He also tightened inside with a need to make her tell more than what the detectives had written down, and to tell him why, if nothing else, he ached for her to tell him why.

CHAPTER 19

"**G**one where?" Jimmy yelled and pushed past old Horsnell. He ducked under the wide leather belts that ran from the mill wheel to the wooden gears, and to the flywheel and iron shafts that drove the saw blade up and down. "Where did they go?"

"She won't tell, that bitch of a woman," Horsnell griped. He hung a lantern on a nail peg. "Folk been talking against what she's been doing. Some were here today asking about you and your sisters."

Jimmy stopped at the gleaming saw blade, which he had sharpened many times under Horsnell's care. "Who was here?"

"Church folk."

Horsnell limped over to the saw blade. A helpless Methuselah who had once bragged that he had set the teeth on crosscut saws that had knocked down the biggest masts for the biggest ships in the world.

"Times change," he offered by way of excuse for having been silent when Jimmy had been bonded away. "They're talking now. Some anyway. Ever since what happened to the Fagan girl up at the Parker place. Grace Fagan laid charges against Bobby Parker and Sam Nelson, but nobody could prove nothing. It was Grace's word against theirs."

Jimmy stamped his foot and turned away.

Horsnell continued. "That's how come she bonds them far away from here."

"Where?" Jimmy spun on Horsnell.

"New Brunswick. Quebec. Ontario, maybe. I don't know!"

Jimmy kicked through a pile of sawdust as he remembered how Miss Golding had paraded him and others before the congregation of St. Boniface Church in Aylesford and had sweetly bragged about the good she was doing her children. "Hiring out the boys for farm work and the girls for household cleaning and scrubbing," she had said. Father Morton had stood next to her, nodding his approval. "It will teach them the value of hard work."

"What happened to Grace, could happen to Robina and Annie," Jimmy said.

Horsnell dropped his eyes.

Jimmy shook all over to think it. "That bitch of a woman," he snarled. "She'll tell me." He bolted from the sawmill, skirted the water wheel, and crossed the rickety wooden bridge at the narrow end of the head pond.

"It's been too long," Horsnell muttered to himself and shifted over to the sawmill door. He hollered, "It's been too long, Jimmy. Too long."

Jimmy climbed from Graves Brook and turned toward the main house on the hilltop. He picked his way through the orchard with the blossoms budding out, then slipped among the elm trees and maples that surrounded the house. He leaped onto the back porch and entered the kitchen, crouching through the downstairs to find Miss Golding in the front parlour, Bible-reading. She sat stiff and straight in a Windsor rocker, pooled in lamplight. Her hair hung in braids over the shoulders of her pale blue housecoat. Her eyes were set hard and tight to her nose, her face droopy from sleep, her lips tightened to a slit that almost suggested a smile.

Side tables and wooden chairs were conveniently scattered about the room at different angles, as though to sharpen one's attention to the activity in hand — knitting, reading, sewing, needlepoint. A large, gilt-framed painting of men scything a hayfield and woman gathering hay and piling it into conical stacks hung above a mantel that framed the bricked recess for a cast-iron pot-bellied stove. Samplers decorated the opposite wall. Two bow windows filled out the room, and these were heavy with dark blue drapes with yellow cords.

Jimmy made himself big in the doorway. "Where did you send them?"

Miss Golding stopped rocking, marked her place in the Book of Deuteronomy, and drilled Jimmy with her eyes. "I see you have run away, James Delaney. Well, you had your chance."

"I want my sisters."

"They are not here." Her mocking voice worked his anger. "Unlike you, Robina and Annie are making the most of the opportunity I have given them. They're happy for it."

"Tell me where they are, or I'll . . ."

"You'll what? What will you do, James Delaney? Threaten me and run off? That's as much as you can do. A temperament passed down from father to son."

Jimmy's mind blurred. He looked for something to set his hands on. Books. Planter. Porcelain vase. Fire tools beside the stove.

"A wastrel when your father cast you off and now an ungrateful runaway and a common bully."

His body coiled and he lunged at her. His fists swung wildly. One knocked the Bible from her hands. The other struck an oil lamp and sent it flying from the table. It smashed on the floor and caught the drapes on fire.

Miss Golding screamed.

Jimmy panicked and bolted from the house. He ran through the stand of elm and maple, and through the apple orchard. He did not look back until he reached the meadow beyond Graves Brook and the dam that backed up the head pond for the mill. He saw the flames licking up the front of the house. He crouched and held his stomach and started to cry.

CHAPTER 20

At Dempsey's Corner, where the road turned right, Delaney stopped to take his bearings. The clear night had grown cold. He hunched into his heavy canvas coat and walked on, a mile, until he heard the steady rumble of the mill wheel turning. The splash of water. Through the trees, he saw light from the sawmill and the silhouette of a man in the open double doors. He heard the man call out something unintelligible, then break into a hobbled run. Delaney watched the man run past the mill wheel, across a rickety wooden foot-bridge, and up a sloping field.

Through the tree branches, Delaney saw an orange light growing ever brighter. He splashed through the mountain runoff. He now had a clear view of the main house at Hillside Farm. It was on fire.

By the time he got there, flames engulfed the parlour and another front room. They were reaching upward to the bedrooms on the second floor. The dry timbers, floor planks, and clapboard walls burned like tinder.

The children, all in their nightshirts, watched from beside the stable. Their terrified faces were red from the heat. In the pupils of their wide eyes were individual tongues of fire.

Delaney ordered three boys to fetch water buckets from the stable and fill them at the well. He then directed the older boys and girls into two lines for passing full buckets forward and empty ones back. He saw the man from the sawmill hobble across the farmyard and to the well. He remembered the man's name was Horsnell. Miss Golding doubled over on the ground beside the well. She coughed smoke from her lungs. She pointed to the upstairs of the house and said something to Horsnell.

Delaney tossed buckets of water toward the base of the fire. Suddenly, the entire front of the house burst into flame.

Horsnell was now beside him. Above the windstorm of flames firing through the downstairs, Horsnell shouted, "She left two little girls up there!"

Delaney's frightened eyes went from Horsnell to the fire and then to Miss Golding crouched beside the well. His hands trembled. Water spilled from the bucket.

Horsnell grabbed his arm and shouted. "Try!"

Delaney started for the summer kitchen, stopped on the back stoop, and doused himself with a bucket of water. He threw the door, and the fire exploded from the parlour and down the narrow hall straight at him. He ducked from the kitchen to the stoop and rolled to the ground, hugging it and shaking all over.

Horsnell ran to the stoop and doused him with two more buckets. He knelt and took Delaney's face in his hands. "The stairs are straight off the kitchen."

Delaney hesitated. His face tight with fear.

Horsnell pulled at his arm. "Go! For Christ sakes, go!"

Delaney crawled across the stoop and into the kitchen. He kept low to escape the smoke and flames, and to suck the air that the fire was drawing along the floor through the open kitchen door. Still low, he swirled at the centre of the room, straining through stinging eyes to find the stairs to the second floor. Flames were up the kitchen walls and flaring across the ceiling. He saw the stairs. On hands and knees he climbed through the choking smoke and under an archway of flames.

The closed door at the head of the stairs was hot to his touch. He drew a deep breath, held it, and reached for the knob. The scorched metal burned his hand and burned out his held breath. He screamed and threw open the door.

A blast of smoke blinded him and stuffed his lungs. For an instant he held fire in his arms then tossed it aside. He flattened on the floor. Beneath the smoke and flames, he saw two tiny, terrified faces pressed into a corner with the paint bubbling off the walls.

He crawled and crawled across the floor that was smoking and smouldering from the fire burning in the kitchen below. When he reached the girls, the bubbling paint burst into flames. He gathered them crying into his arms, shielding them with his big body. He straightened and ran for the stairs.

The smoke caught him choking on the way down. He stumbled and skidded off the treads, broadening his shoulders to steady himself between the fiery walls of the stairway. In the kitchen, fire burned up his back and over his neck. He ran across the kitchen, through the open door, and over the fiery stoop.

Horsnell caught him and guided him away from the burning building. He grabbed a filled bucket and doused the fire on Delaney's back.

Delaney choked up smoke from his lungs. He drew air and coughed it out, then another, and another. He coughed and coughed. Then he rolled to his side, and unfolded the two children safely from his arms.

The old man fell to his knees and squealed. "God Almighty, man!"

Flames roared through the roof. The house seemed to shake with the heat, then buckle. Iron nails turned bright blue and exploded like gunshots.

Delaney lay on the ground coughing and gasping, aching to get air into his lungs. The burns on his hands and back were agony. Despite the intense heat, he was shivering.

There was a loud, painful groan from the burning trusses and timbers. The roof collapsed.

CHAPTER 21

Reverend Morton's wife treated Delaney's hands and back with an apothecary's unguent, which she used for stove burns. She gently wrapped his hands in swaddling and said, "Miss Golding accused your son of starting the fire."

Delaney nodded. He felt the pain from the burning now that the shock of it had worn off.

"But Horsnell said different," she continued. She ripped a strip of swaddling and used it to loosely tie the bandages on Delaney's hands. "He said it was an accident. He said someone, he would not say who, had set a lamp too close to the curtains. What did Sheriff Fletcher tell you?"

Delaney shook his head and thanked her for nursing his burns.

Delaney's hands healed into a scar all twisted about like baggy-wrinkle. His neck and back looked much the same.

Rufus DeWolfe of Stewiacke looked at the brown ripples on Delaney's neck and asked him to say his name again. Delaney obliged and DeWolfe slammed the door on him, but not before calling Delaney's son "a lazy bastard."

When Delaney went to John and Agnes Tuttle's white two-storey house overlooking the Pugwash harbour, Agnes had said she did not know what he was talking about. She had never heard of Miss Golding of Hillside Farm and never had two girls employed in her house.

The postman told Delaney a girl and young woman had worked as house servants for the Tuttles. It must be two years ago. They didn't work there long, six months, maybe eight.

Delaney went back to Tuttle's house. John Tuttle met him at the door with an old muzzle-loading horse pistol. Delaney backed off.

CHAPTER 22

Robina walked to keep walking, the road going on
and on. Walking barefoot or in those damn wooden
shoes Madame LeBlanc had given her. Walking out
her life. Losing her way and going deep inside herself. Down that
tunnel where the sadness was too dark to see her way out. No
Annie to follow her down. No Annie to take her hand and lead
her into sunshine.

"Annie," she called out from a dream. Curled against a stone
wall and wide-eyed at the startling cry of wild geese overhead.
Cows mooed from a nearby pasture.

She drank from a cold stream. She removed her dusty clothes
and washed in the stream. She avoided seeing herself in the water.

She walked for ages in her grey floppy hat with the brim
folded back, and with the apple-picker's basket over her shoulder
and tied at the waist. Town to village, village to town. Closed
doors. Closed hearts. The streets rolled up against what one

shopkeeper had called "a horde of beggars," and what a woman had said were "paupers and Lazzaroni come here to torment us." Churches shut tight. The parsonage shuttered. A crucifix like a fingerboard pointing both ways out of town.

The road led along a rail line and through a long stretch of black stumps and briars. She rested on a boulder. Silent and sober. No sound among the charred mullein stalks and goldenrod. Thin light half-reflected off the scorched land.

That night, in a field of scythed hay, she bedded down beside a family with their lives in patches. The mother had wild red hair, the father a bony face and tolerant eyes. The children were scarecrows in three different sizes.

"This country is on its knees and crawling," the woman said.

Robina half-listened as she scouted for a place to lie down.

"Coming together did no good," the woman continued. "That Macdonald, the head of it all, talking big."

"Depression, some are calling it," the man said.

"And he's shouting for a railway," the woman said.

The man shook his head.

Robina found the spot she was looking for. She gathered hay for her bed.

"We been walking our hearts out," the man said. "There's nothing for no one. We'll walk ourselves to death."

"You will too," the woman said to Robina. "The way things are, we'll all walk until our souls turn black."

The next day they travelled together until they arrived at a fork in the road. The family followed the road that crossed a plank bridge and turned out of sight. Robina continued travelling as straight a course as possible. Her road ran parallel to a whitewashed, four-board fence. She looked down the line of the fence to where it and the road converged into a single streak that went on forever.

Some people she met said Toronto. They said it was the city at the end of things. Others said west. They said it was the beginning.

She wondered how far there was to go, knowing there was no real place she was looking for. She was just going. Afraid that whatever was behind her was catching up. She grew hungry and ate shrunken raspberries she found along the roadside. She piled coloured leaves against the trunk of a wide maple and sat against it. She heard small animals in the underwood. She heard the tall trees groan in the breeze.

She walked herself into another winter and into the barnyard of a sour old woman and a crippled old man.

The two of them were haggard and austere. He was hammering battens over wide cracks in the boards on the north side of the house. She banked straw bundles against the fieldstone foundation. Her movements were slow and unsure. Her face thin and pasty.

Robina begged for food and a night in the barn.

The old woman grumbled something under her breath. She turned to Robina. "You know how to work?"

Together they wove the straw bundles into a thatch that would bank the snow to keep the cold wind from blowing through the stone foundation.

"A cold floor and what's stored below has the bejesus frozen out of it," the old woman said. She coughed deep and choked back what came up.

Robina saw pain in the old woman's eyes. A look she had seen in her mother's face. "I banked a house before," she said.

"Where was that?"

"Nova Scotia."

"Nova Scotia," the old woman snarled. "It don't get the cold we get. It don't get the snow either." She looked at the thatch work over the foundation. Pleased with it. "A day's work for the hay barn and meals. Stay longer and work off the winter if you want. Fair trade."

Robina settled into the barn. For her keep, she chopped firewood for a cookstove and heater, churned when there was cream worth churning, fed and watered the cow and horse and two sheep. She mucked out the stalls wearing the old woman's gumboots.

One cold January morning, she and Mr. Davies rode a flatbed sleigh to the frozen pond about a mile down a snow-covered woods road. She wore one of his old blanket coats, a knitted wool hat, and knitted wool socks on her hands. They got out and walked on the pond with their legs apart and their toes splayed inside felt-lined boots. Robina carried a measured length of rope and an ice pick. The old man carried an auger and the four-foot-long ice saw. He went back to the sleigh for two sets of ice tongs and a shovel.

They cleared a large patch of snow, then marked out four two-by-five-foot blocks. Davies augered a saw hole in a corner of each of them. He sawed through ice that was ten to twelve inches thick. He sawed the long sides of the block. Robina sawed the short ones.

"Don't force it," Davies explained. "Stand straight and get a rhythm going with your knees. Let the ice saw do the work." He demonstrated from a distance, having already experienced her reluctance at working side by side with a man.

Once when it was her turn to saw, he stood aside and smoked a black briar pipe. He talked around the pipe in his mouth and over the grind and scrape of the saw. He talked with the need to talk. He seemed not to expect a response from Robina. He talked like someone accustomed to talking to himself, she thought, in a voice gnawed with remorse.

"I been harvesting ice since I was tall enough to work the ice saw," he said. "My father and me. My brother when he got old enough. He got killed working a steam freighter down in Lake Erie."

He drew on the pipe and blew smoke.

"Time tells a tale about all of us," he said. "It tells a tale about you. A woman your age. It's not my business, I know. Wondering is all I'm doing. I had a son who run off. We cut ice together. We did most work on the farm together. We had words and got into something. I can't remember who said what. I doubt he remembers. Maybe he does. Maybe I do. That's the way of it. It took me years to learn that blame is a hard rule to live by. I got no idea where he run to."

Robina finished sawing. He broke the block free with the pick. They cut three more blocks. With the tongs they hauled each block from the water and floated them over the sheeted ice to the shore.

"Mrs. Davies never could've done this with me," he said. "The grippe got hold of her last winter and it never let go."

He rigged up a rope and pulley to a tree limb. Robina fetched leather straps from the sleigh. They fitted the straps around an ice block and lifted it onto the sleigh. They lifted the other blocks the same way.

At the farm, Davies had a contraption for lifting the blocks from the sleigh to a shoot that sloped into the ice house. They covered the blocks with sawdust.

That night the wind through the barn was unmerciful. Mr. Davies invited Robina to sit with them beside the Morning Glory heater. Mrs. Davies squinted over needlepoint. The lamp beside her smoked from having the wick turned up too high. The shadow of her hands danced on the walls.

The wind rattled the windows and coughed smoke back down the chimney. Mr. Davies opened the damper on the stove a little at a time with each blast of wind.

"We'll burn through a pile of wood," he said. "Deep cold is setting in."

He went to the shed and came back with an armload of boards, a hammer, and a mouthful of nails. In no time, he framed a small cot beside the stove.

Mrs. Davies sent him for a tick their son had slept on.

"You tend the fire," she told Robina. She went upstairs to bed. Mr. Davies went soon after.

Robina stoked the fire and loaded in a length of rock maple and one of yellow birch. She stripped to her petticoat and lay on the cot under a threadbare bolster. Cuddled in the warmth, she fell asleep thinking of Annie.

One night, Mrs. Davies set aside her needlepoint and hummed a song Robina remembered her mother singing in the Irish language. When the old woman broke into a deep-throated cough, Robina picked up the tune, humming and singing a few words in Irish.

In the morning, Mrs. Davies remained in bed. She coughed and choked and cried out for the pain that ravaged her insides.

Robina brought her tea and helped her sit up to drink it. Two sips and the old woman had had enough. Robina laid her back down. The old woman's grey hair splayed over the pillow. Robina saw the old woman's pained and ghostly face, and her frightened eyes. She saw her dying mother laying in that bed, and Annie standing beside it, holding their mother's hand and asking, "How many miles to Babylon?"

Robina never again took tea to the old woman. When the spring rains played out, she helped Mr. Davies harness the horse to a bent plough.

"It ploughs crooked," he said, laughing. "But crooked's good enough for the time being."

He sensed Robina had something to say and stood there itching for her to say it.

She looked at him. She looked at the house. "I can't stay here and watch her die," she said.

His shoulders sunk and he reached for her, then pulled back.

"It's hard," he said. "It's been all I can take. I doubt I can take much more."

She went to the house and gathered what little she owned.

He loaded her apple-picker's basket with grub, a few days' worth, more if she rationed it.

She walked from the farmyard to the road and turned in the direction she had been walking when she had first arrived. She never looked back.

The walking was easier in the worn leather boots the old man had given her. Blackflies swarmed and damn near drove her crazy. She climbed a snake fence and up a hill to an open field where a breeze blew off the flies. At night the mosquitoes took their turn. She hunkered in the blanket coat the old man had given her. She cried herself to sleep.

CHAPTER 23

On a cool October morning, Jimmy Delaney, Gabby Baker, and Henry Kitchen rode a freight wagon up the Nashwaak River to join a logging crew near Stanley, New Brunswick. They hopped off and started walking eight miles into the bush. Gabby knew the way to the logging camp.

Gabby and Henry were older than Jimmy. He had just turned twenty, filled out in his chest and arms, a lot stronger from when he slaved for Rufus DeWolfe. Henry, tall and solid, sported a beard. Gabby and Jimmy had chops. They all wore larrigans to the knees and thick wool pants. Henry and Gabby had met the night before at Mag the Hag's unlicensed saloon in Fredericton. Jimmy they met on the road outside Devon.

Gabby and Henry walked and bragged about the hangover they suffered and the time they had with two of Mag's girls. Jimmy listened.

"Paying makes it right," Henry was saying. "You don't look back on them girls."

"I wouldn't mind seeing the one I had," Gabby said.

"You can't look back on no girl," Henry emphasized. "Otherwise they claw you into hell and you won't never get out."

"Not all of them," Gabby said. "Not the ones back home. I got one I like a lot."

"She'll have you running scared. They all got nails on them like nothing you never seen. I know what I'm talking about. They're back scratch wild one day and go stubborn the next. I got one with a bellyful, but you think I'm looking back? Not for nothing. You look back and all you see is what's done and over. There ain't nothing you can do about what's behind you. I look straight ahead. That's what I do."

Jimmy listened, mulling it over. At last he said to Henry, "You got to marry her. "

"I don't got to do nothing," Henry said. "I don't even know it was me. Jane Willard could've been running goods for half the boys in that town."

"What town?" Gabby demanded, like he could not believe there was a hometown with girls like that.

"Cornwall, Ontario," Henry said. "Go there, and you're going nowhere."

Jimmy stopped, and the other two stopped. "You can't just leave her that way," Jimmy insisted.

"I'll leave her anyway I want," bragged Henry.

"It's not right."

"It is for me." Henry winked at Gabby. "You're all full of what's right to do."

"Some things are that way," Jimmy said.

"Well, if it's so right, why don't you marry her?

Gabby snickered.

Henry pressed, "You don't have a girl, none you said you had. You should marry her. Yeah, do her right and marry her."

Henry laughed and walked on. Gabby followed him. The two of them nattered on for miles.

Jimmy walked in silence. Thinking. He strayed to the side of the road, taken by the camouflage of colour.

They hit a stretch so brilliant it appeared to be on fire. Jimmy stopped and gazed at it. The other two stopped and looked back at him.

"A fellow could walk ten yards off either side and disappear," Jimmy said.

Gabby and Henry exchanged looks and shrugged.

"I could too," Henry boasted. "I could walk out the other side of the goddamn world."

The camp smelled of spruce gum and mud mixed with horse manure. There were twenty or so Clydesdales and Percherons inside a paddock built of logs interlaced with spruce boughs. Someone pointed them to the camp office and to the "Main John," the loggers' name for the boss of the operation.

The Main John was a tall, thin man with a white beard and ice in his eyes. His name was Simon Booth. He sat behind a plank table. He leaned his chair against the log wall of his office and carefully studied the three of them, judging whether they were fit for lumberjack work, at chopping and sawing in the bush, or skidding logs to the yard and loading the heavy sleds for the teamsters to drive to the riverbank. He needed liners and rossers to chalk-line and notch-measure the logs for the hewers, who could skin off fourteen inches with each stroke of a broad axe, then smooth the surface as if it had been planed.

Gabby pulled off his cap.

"What's your name?" Simon Booth asked.

"Gabby Baker."

"You know logging work?"

"I know it. Worked a McQuire camp last year."

Simon Booth wrote Gabby's name into a cloth-bound book. Gabby smiled at Henry and Jimmy.

Henry was next, smiling through his hungover face. That larky look in his eyes.

"You?" Booth growled to look at him.

"Kitchen. Henry Kitchen."

"You know about logging work?"

"Not much."

The Main John fixed him solid. "Not much, or nothing?"

"Nothing."

The Main John wiped his face to a scowl. "Learning will harden muscles that ain't never been hard. You're big enough to work the woods. Only question is whether you're tough enough."

Henry shuffled. "I can do it. I know I can."

Simon Booth harrumphed and wrote Henry's name in the book. He turned to Jimmy. "What's your name?"

"Jimmy."

Booth scowled. "Jimmy what?"

Jimmy started to say his last name but stopped short. Still worried about the house fire at Hillside Farm. Then he said it. "Delaney, my name is Jimmy Delaney.

"You sure?"

"It's my name. I should know my own name."

"Yea, you should, but you don't say it like it's yours. You running from something?"

Jimmy looked off the Main John to Gabby and Henry. Jimmy shook his head. "I got nothing to run about."

"You hiding? You won't be the first. Plenty think they can hole away in a logging camp. You one of them?"

"I got nothing to hide about."

"Nothing, huh? You know about logging work?"

"I done it. Worked a camp outside Grand Falls and a woodlot outside Truro. I know saw filing and mill work."

"Where'd you learn it?"

"A mill sawyer named Horsnell."

"Andy Horsnell?"

Jimmy nodded.

"Darn good man," Booth reminisced. "Last I heard, Horsnell was milling lumber in some work home for boys. That was years ago." Booth started to write Jimmy's name in the book then stopped. He lifted his eyes. "Did you live in that home?"

Jimmy shrugged and dropped his chin.

Simon Booth looked Jimmy over good. "There's no shame in that. What was that last name you gave?"

"Delaney."

"Delaney. Well, Jimmy Delaney, if I hear the sour sound of just one saw, you'll be dragging those dull teeth until your stomach splits. The saw gang'll be dinnering out about now. See Mrs. Darrow to get a bite, then get to work. And you!" The Main John again drilled Henry Kitchen. "Tell the Bull Push you're green."

❧

They found the saw gang about a mile in the bush. The Bull Push assigned Gabby to a crosscut saw with another fellow, and Henry to a water wagon, from which he would fill buckets and lug them to the fifty or so sawyers knocking down trees.

Jimmy carried the sharpening tools in a leather pouch and travelled from one gang to another. He tuned off the dull notes that played from crosscuts and bucksaws. The sawyers welcomed him. A few mocked his skinny frame, a sapling in a forest of big trees. Most just appreciated his skill for easing their work and the simple way he would notch a stump and shim it for holding a saw blade upside down for filing.

The boys were dog-tired when they hit the camp house that first night. They sat together and, for the most part, ate in silence. Then Gabby dug out a scrap of salt pork from his plate of beans, scoffed it down without chewing, and made a sucking sound with his lips.

"Delaney your real name?" Gabby challenged.

Henry lifted his eyes from his plate and looked at Jimmy.

Jimmy didn't move. He didn't answer.

"I'm just wondering, that's all," Gabby said. "It just seemed funny the way you didn't say it to Henry and me, and the way you didn't say it to the Main John right off. Like you was trying to think one up."

Jimmy forked himself a mouthful of beans, then stabbed a biscuit in the juice and ate that too. He looked at both of them squarely. "It's my name. I say it when I want."

Jimmy and Gabby shared a bunk with a single straw tick. Jimmy had little to say that night and even less in the morning when they washed up at the two-man sink. For the next few days, Jimmy spoke to Gabby and Henry only when he had to. Evenings he kept to himself.

Gabby, on the other hand, could talk the bunkhouse deaf. He'd go on and on about one foolish thing after another — boxing matches with bunkhouse fleas, a cook drinking himself drunk on Catawba wine and boiling up salt beef without soaking it. He told about a former slave who slipped his chains and tracked north and now runs a log drive on the St. John River. He told about a Nova Scotia forest that disappears at night. The men laughed at what Gabby said and the gawky way he said it. They laughed with him.

Henry Kitchen they laughed at, both behind his back and to his face. They called him a whiner, because he was a steady stream of complaint, mostly about tromping the bush with two six-quart buckets stretching out his arms, making rounds to the men, all chewing tobacco and dribbling, scooping a pint, sipping and dumping it back so as to scum up the water in the buckets. It made Henry sick to look at it. He complained about having to keep refilling the buckets. He complained about his wages too, the length of his bunk, and the bunkhouse stink. He complained about the food, and that set Mrs. Darrow and her husband against him. Several times he swore he had had enough with tangling his legs in slash and tripping over junked-up trees. And once when a dropped tree fell sideways, bounced, and nearly caught him in the legs, he promised those within earshot that he would be gone from camp in the morning. Yet he stuck it out. Some laughed and wondered how long he would last. Others said Henry was too goddamn scared to run.

One morning, Gabby fetched Jimmy from the bush to sharpen a whipsaw the camp gang had jig-mounted on an elevated platform for sawing up boards for a new floor in the cookhouse. They returned to camp, where two sawyers were painfully cutting through a log, the dull blade hauling out their guts.

Tom Farrell stood on top of the platform and Teddy Buchanan below. Farrell wore canvas clothes that were sweat-stained and covered with wood shavings. He had a stubble face and wore a soft peaked cap that he held on with a leather chinstrap. Buchanan wore woollen pants and black braces. He had a thick black beard and wore a slouch hat. Shavings stuck in his beard.

They pulled and pushed, up and down, in a syncopated rhythm that could only be matched by a man and wife who had been a long time married. A runty man named Ian Cassidy inched the log forward on oiled wooden rails as the sawyers slowly sawed through the length of it.

When they were done cutting, Jimmy ordered the sawyers to remove the saw from the jig and fix it in a wooden vise. He unfolded his leather pouch on the newly cut beam. He eyed the beam closely to determine the angle and heaviness of how the blade was cutting and how it needed sharpening. From pockets in the pouch, Jimmy slid out a tooth gauge to set the rakers and cutting teeth to the right height, flat files for sharpening the cutters, a swage for gauging the thickness of the grooves between teeth, and a set hammer.

Gabby rolled a log in place, and sat to see over Jimmy's right shoulder. Farrell, Buchanan, and Cassidy gathered close as well.

"Henry hates you knowing how to set saw teeth," Gabby said. "Me too!"

Jimmy filed the length of the saw blade. He checked the teeth and nodded. "Proof's in the sawing."

He and Gabby unclamped the saw from the vise, and Gabby climbed up the platform with the saw. He passed one end down to Jimmy. They started into a new log. The rhythm was off on Jimmy's side.

"I should've known you can't saw," Gabby teased.

They gave the saw over to the sawyers to finish the log and stood beside the platform and watched.

"How long it take you to learn?" Gabby asked.

"A couple of years to get it right," Jimmy said without taking his eyes from the sawyers. "I learned milling too."

Jimmy remembered old Horsnell teaching him how to saw prime logs with a tight grain into quarter-sawn boards. He remembered Horsnell carefully wedging logs for straight, clean cuts, his white hair wispy in the breeze from the mill wheel turning and the stroking blade.

Horsnell had been a nail of a man, always talking around the stumpy pipe in his mouth, telling stories about his days in the woods, and about a time he had travelled west and the woods had played out to a flat, open land where the wind was steady, like the breath of a woman hungry for love. "Unfenced land," Horsnell had called it, "running on forever. And hot in summer, fry your arse whenever you sat down. But hot for nothing to the cold in winter, with a wind that blew your piss to ice before it stained the snow."

Horsnell had regretted not going back to that land and the sod house with a woman in a flour apron. He had said it more times than Jimmy could count. "The woods are a wonder, boy, but the prairie is the kind of place where a man could leave his mark on the world. Make something of his self."

The sawyers stopped sawing, and Farrell hollered down to Jimmy, "It saws good."

"I can hear that," Jimmy hollered back. He gathered his tools in the leather pouch.

Gabby walked him back into the bush. "You learn saw filing at that place?"

Jimmy nodded.

"I heard they beat you in places like that," Gabby pressed. "I don't know where I heard it, but I did. They beat you?"

Jimmy said nothing.

"You don't want to say?"

"I'd say if they did."

They walked a quarter mile through clear-cut that was strewn with stubble and stumps. They could hear the saws now. They could hear the axes banging U-shaped dogs into felled trees for hitching a team to for skidding logs clear of the woods for yarding. The whole time Jimmy said nothing. They bypassed a burning pile of slash, then Jimmy stopped and looked at the fire.

"They beat me," Jimmy confessed. He gathered an armful of slash and tossed it to the flames. "Not much. Twice. Some did worse than beating you. She did, anyway. Miss Golding." He lowered his head and his voice lowered with it. "She sold us, my sisters and me. Others. She sold us to work on farms."

Gabby tightened his eyes on Jimmy and pursed his lips like a hungry man when the juice is running. "So you run off?"

Jimmy remembered standing outside the window of the big house at Hillside Farm and seeing Miss Golding in the parlour with the flames running up the curtains and the walls. He swallowed hard and showed Gabby a pointed look. His voice tried for cold but broke apart with feeling. "I run all right. I been running."

"They can't do nothing for running off," Gabby said. "Growing up makes amends for a lot of what we done. I go home, and it's Gabby this and Gabby that. But I won't settle there. I got a girl, and we'll go off somewhere else. You ever want to go back and see that place?"

Jimmy shook his head. "It's not there no more. It burned down."

⌘

The woods froze, and the saw gangs cut sled roads anticipating the snow. Jimmy reduced the set of the saw teeth on every damn saw in the whole damn camp. Frozen wood does not require as much set as wood thawed and running with resin. He worked evenings at a vise in the blacksmith shop to catch up. Gabby helped.

When it finally did snow, it was non-stop for three days. Strong winds shut down the operation, imprisoning the men in the bunkhouse to arm-wrestle and swap stories. Gabby was in his glory. His grandfather had been a talker and Gabby remembered most stories his grandfather had told.

"There was an evangelist named Sojourner Coleman," Gabby started. "A real soul-saver."

Jimmy sat forward on his bunk and smiled at how Gabby could tone his voice to draw his audience in.

"Coleman hit Cambridge Narrows, a village on Washademoak Lake, in mid-February," Gabby told. "They were hard-working people there. Farmers scratching out a meagre living. House full of kids. They were hard-living folks thereabouts, folks with a crying need for salvation and no church or preacher of their own.

"Coleman spread the word that he would satisfy that need on Sunday, outside Enos Blackie's coach house. Come Sunday morning, and Coleman climbed on a sleigh, waved his hands for attention, and called on Jesus Christ to join them for spiritual healing."

Gabby paused and looked into the faces of his fellow loggers. "We all been there," he said. "We all know the heartache of sin."

Several men raised both hands and said, "Amen."

"Amen, amen," Gabby repeated. He lowered his voice. "'Amen to those who trust in the Lord,' Coleman demanded. 'Amen to those scoured out by the ravages of sin.' Coleman struck a pose like that of Moses exhibiting the Ten Commandments. Then he let loose into a storm of fire and brimstone. Every soul gathered about lowered their heads in the hard and fast belief that evil had tainted them at one time or another. Coleman had them primed for a cleansing, and for digging silver from their pockets and purses for the privilege of being cleansed. He led those sinners from the village and out on the lake, where two men had axed a wide hole in the ice. Coleman called it the 'holy hole.'"

Again Gabby paused. He shook his head sadly and said, "The first candidate for baptism was an elderly woman named Eleanor Bradshaw. She slipped and slid across the ice and Coleman took both her hands to steady her.

"'Do you take Jesus as your saviour?'

"Mrs. Bradshaw nodded.

"As Coleman dipped her in the holy hole, he lost his footing as well as his grip on Mrs. Bradshaw. She disappeared under the ice. Those on shore gasped.

"Coleman turned to the gathering and said, 'The Lord giveth and the Lord taketh away. Hand me another one.'"

Jimmy laughed, along with most of the loggers.

Then Gabby told about Frank Jones, a young logger from Stanley Bridge who got a taste of the big city from a painted-face woman named Phoebe Duckshire.

"Oh my sweet heaven, wasn't Phoebe Duckshire a woman of the world," Gabby crowed. "A woman who knew the price of everything she was selling. And what she was selling weren't fine leather gloves or buttons and bows. She charged Frank Jones for keeping him company. They walked along the waterfront. That cost Frank a dollar. They sat on a bench and held hands. That cost a dollar more. The night Phoebe took Frank home cost him whatever was left in the purse he carried. Then Frank discovered Phoebe charged other men for the same overnight favour!"

Gabby looked around at the faces eager for him to continue telling. Then he said, "There's not one of us here that does not know the power of a woman to savage a man's heart with the goods she's selling. No doubt in my mind, no doubt at all."

Teddy Buchanan crossed his arms. "Tell us what happened."

Gabby took an even longer look around the bunkhouse. "The next morning, Frank started out for Stanley Bridge, his heart bleeding with every step he took. Then, all of a sudden he turned back. He was all teary-eyed as he stood outside Phoebe's house. Then he started sobbing and set her house on fire."

That reminded an old logger named Finney about a man named Brewster who set his own house on fire, losing his wife and three kids in the blaze.

Teddy Buchanan said, "A few winters ago a school of some kind, an orphanage in Nova Scotia, burned down. Nobody died, but someone got burned bad."

Another man told another story about a house burning. As he spoke, Jimmy eased his way from his bunk and left the bunkhouse. Gabby followed him through the piling snow for the blacksmith shed. Jimmy fixed a saw blade in the vise and sharpened so hard he damn near wore a single cutter to a nub.

The blacksmith was at the forge pumping the bellows for a blast of heat. His eyes gleamed and his cheeks reddened from the hot glow that highlighted the spotted grey in his dark beard and close-cropped dark hair. He trimmed the coals with a poker, readying them to puddle iron for hammering. He reached for the wooden shaft and pumped again. The coals in the forge whitened like a soul in pain. A few shook in the heavy draft from the bellows and shattered in their own heat.

"I could use a hand," the blacksmith said to Jimmy and Gabby.

They helped him iron clad the wooden runners on a hauling sled. They pried the hot iron band over a runner, hammered it to fit, then let it cool and tighten around the curved wood.

The blacksmith returned to the forge to heat another iron band.

Gabby started to nose a file across the saw blade in the vise and stopped at the cutter Jimmy had filed. He sighted along the blade, then leaned close and fingered the teeth one by one, taking his time. He lifted his eyes to Jimmy, who was simply staring at the glowing coals in the forge.

The blacksmith stopped pumping. "We'll have to catch up after this," the blacksmith said. He gestured with his narrow chin toward the window at the blowing snow. "They'll be hauling when they shouldn't be. Busting runners."

When the wind had settled, Simon Booth had the saw gangs knocking down twice their quota, dulling blades. Jimmy ploughed knee-deep from one gang to another. He also took his turn with the sand hill men spreading sand on the icy sled road so the teamsters could haul twice as many loads.

The sled was a criss-cross of squared timbers stretched across thick wooden, ironclad runners. The load of logs ran lengthwise across the timbers and parallel to the runners. The trick was to stack a load no higher than the sled was wide. Some teamsters over-stacked their sleds. Nolan Carston over-stacked his late one afternoon.

"Save that load for morning," Teddy Buchanan told him.

"I got making up to do," Carston said. "I'm down two loads in wages."

"You can't team in the dark," Teddy said.

Carston climbed high on the hauling sled and took the reins. "I can team with my eyes closed."

Jimmy, Gabby, and Henry scampered to where the sled road cut a narrow turn to avoid the marsh at the base of the bluff. They set up where the sled road turned the sharpest, and the sidehill dropped thirty feet down a slope into a ravine. They lit coal-oil cans and spaced them along the roadside. They built a bonfire to warm the sand and waited. They listened for the harness rattling and the crack of a blacksnake whip. To hear it meant the sled was coming.

Six others went to the start of the turn to sand the ice to slow the hauling sled after it caught speed on the downhill run.

"He should have strapped a brake chain around those runners," said a logger at the head of the turn, his voice carrying a long way through the winter woods.

The heavy load reached the top of the hill and started down. Nolan stood on top of the logs with the traces wrapped around his left wrist. His belted coat flapped around his legs. He cracked the whip a couple of times and whooped to keep the horses galloping out ahead of the heavy sled. The runners grabbed in spots where the ice surface had been well sanded, and shot ahead where it wasn't.

Jimmy, Henry, and Gabby started sanding the sharpest part of the turn. They sanded the inside first, then they crossed over and sanded where the runners would swing wide and threaten the edge of the deep ravine.

All at once in the middle of the downhill run, the overloaded sled started jerking back and forth, catching in the sand on the downhill, then losing the grip on slippery spots. The enormous weight of logs wrenched forward and backward and forward again. More violent with each jerk.

"Listen to that sled," Gabby said. "It's heaving in the turns."

Jimmy looked up hill. "She's coming fast."

"Too fast," Gabby said.

The sled gained speed on a straight stretch. Then the runners hit sand at the start of the sharp turn. They slid on a clear patch and lurched sideways. The load shifted. The runners grabbed sand and squealed. The binding chains on the load let go and the load broke free in a tangle of logs. Carston spilled with the loose logs and fell beneath the timber bunks.

Jimmy jumped across the sled road and printed his body into the snow on the sidehill. He lunged back and grabbed Gabby's coat and yanked him forward. Henry still stood in the path of the oncoming sled. Frozen with fear.

The sled and horses were on them all at once. Jimmy dove for Henry and carried him over the edge and headlong down the slope into the ravine. They tumbled among twisting logs and the scurry of snow flying up. They landed near the bottom, sprawled in a brake of scrub spruce.

Gabby skidded down the slope, followed by Teddy Buchanan. They reached Henry first. He was breathing heavy. His eyes shocked and staring.

Jimmy lay not far away. He rolled to his knees and yelped at a pain that split his back in two. He called to Gabby about Henry.

"He's beat up a bit," Gabby called back and scrambled over. "What about you?"

Jimmy forced a smile and then a laugh. "I'm a goddamn fool."

Others found Carston's body jammed between a timber bunk and an ironclad runner. His head was smashed and his face misshaped beyond recognition. The body was so crushed the men dare not move it until morning.

From their position at the head of the curve, Teddy Buchanan and Learner Michaels had seen it all, and said as much in the bunkhouse that night. Gabby did not hesitate to glorify every one of their words.

Simon Booth gave Jimmy and Henry two days off to ease the ache in their bodies. Henry never moved from his bunk, except to eat. He hardly spoke to anyone, and not a word to Jimmy.

On the second day, Mrs. Darrow called Jimmy into the cook-house, a compliment to any logger invited into her sanctuary of sanctuaries. She stood at the long deal table, her hands tussling with the pile of dough on the bake board. She formed the shaggy mass into a huge ball and started kneading it.

She was a thin woman in a straight brown dress and floury apron. "Feed the stove," she ordered.

Jimmy opened the firebox and loaded in sticks of apple wood and birch.

Mrs. Darrow talked while she kneaded the dough.

"It plays over in your head, doesn't it?"

Jimmy nodded. He poked at the fire to make room for the last stick.

"It works harder on him than it does on you," she continued. "Mr. Darrow knows all about it, and I know it from him. Some men can't tender to living when they should be dead."

Jimmy closed the firebox.

"You made a bargain, you know that, don't you?" she said. "Save a life, owe a life. It's your doing that he and his are now yours for looking after."

Jimmy looked at her.

"Stone hard truth, Jimmy Delaney, and it's bad luck if you don't."

Henry lazed in the bunkhouse for another day, while Jimmy went back to sharpening and trudging through deep snow, which aggravated the ache in his back.

Early the following morning before the bunkhouse woke and the camp bell rang, Jimmy was in the blacksmith's shop sharpening a few dull saws. Through the ice glazed window, he saw someone slinking past. He went to the door and saw Henry Kitchen hurrying down the woods road.

"Where you going? Jimmy hollered.

Henry stopped and turned and hollered back, "As far as I can."

CHAPTER 24

D elaney sat shoulder to shoulder and knees to knees with half a dozen others in a clattering coach. Richmond Hill to Toronto. Three men pipe-smoking, another one chewing and spitting from the window. Delaney breathing hard. His throat and lungs still tight from breathing so much smoke in that house fire. His sweaty hands were fidgety and his eyes panicky because his children's faces escaped his memory.

At a coach stop, he pulled the photograph and studied it. Studied it. Pained to think the passing years had ravaged his memories to a remnant of graveyard faces feeding into his thoughts and dreams, replacing his children's faces. And his wife's.

He rode the rest of the way with the photograph in his hand. Challenging himself to remember more than what he saw in it.

Robina riding the shovel blade as he swirled her round and round over the snow. Her laughing wildly with one hand on the shaft.

Annie in a warm woollen sack Mary had stitched, Delaney proudly holding her high at the shipyard gate so his mates could see his latest.

And Jimmy standing beside him at the canal locks at Lake Banook, watching two men frame a house. Explaining to his son how it's done. Joist by joist, rafter by rafter. Bird-mouth joints at the top plate. A steel square for calculating knee braces.

He got out of the coach at the Front and Yonge Street stop in Toronto, amidst a regiment of shadows chasing him to where he had no sense of where he was. *Just anywhere*, he thought, and smiled to remember the happy face of Murdock Murray. He slogged the mud-sodden streets until the wobbly eyed cow herder at the stockyard pointed and said, "The Ward, a cheapside neighbourhood where some go to disappear."

No lamp, no candles. No window. Just a room with board walls that sucked whatever light slipped through the wide spaces between them. The wind blew through as well. And the snow.

He found work on the waterfront. A dollar and ten cents for a long day of heaving and hauling, but enough to pay his room and board, and tuck some aside.

"Lucky goddamn Irishman landing a job," some said of him.

When they did, he ducked his head and bent his knees to push another cartload of cargo from wharf to warehouse. *Not lucky*, he thought. *Not in what mattered most.*

CHAPTER 25

Jimmy sat on the front steps of the Willard house and stared at the unpainted step between his feet. He had combed his thick brown hair and he smelled of bathwater.

Jane Willard sat on the same step, with her back against a handrail post. She flicked her straw-coloured hair from her pretty round face.

"You don't know that for sure," she insisted.

Jimmy tightened on a feeling sprung from what Horsnell had said about truth sometimes coming with a razor's edge.

"Henry said he'd come back when it got close," she said. "I sent a letter to where he was in Fredericton."

Jimmy winced, knowing Henry had laughed and torn up the letter and thrown it along the road to the logging camp.

Jane looked past Jimmy down the road. "Men . . . Men don't write letters the way women do," she excused.

Jimmy heard the hitch in her voice. He saw her assured expression waver.

From inside the house Mrs. Willard called, "Jane. I need you here."

"Mom," Jane protested.

"Don't you take that tone. You're not too far along to help fix supper."

Jane grumbled something at her mother. She swung her eyes from the door and past Jimmy.

He glanced at her watching down the road. "I'm sure about what he told me and Gabby Baker," he said. "I'm sure he run from the camp and was running as far away as he could run."

Jane's face drained. She turned to him. "He wouldn't say that." She looked back down the road as though looking for something she seemed to fear.

He followed her eyes along a rail fence that slanted through a side field to where the road broke from the treeline to follow the river into town.

"I wouldn't say something mean like that if it wasn't so," he said.

She looked at him, then looked over her shoulder. He followed her eyes through the screened front door and down the long hall to the kitchen, where her mother was stitching a patch on a heavy old coat.

"He wouldn't go like that," she said, her voice fallen off into a question. She felt her belly through her blue cotton dress. She gritted her teeth and looked around for somewhere to settle her eyes. They landed on Jimmy sitting uncomfortable on the stairs and looking at his hands. "He promised," she appealed.

Jimmy looked at her and saw the low sunlight in her eyes. He inhaled the rosewater sweetness that breathed from her hair and from her checker coat and blue cotton dress.

"I'm a saw filer," he said. "I make good wages 'cause a mill can't saw on dull teeth." He wiped his hands on his pants. "I can mill lumber too. I learned milling from old Horsnell. He taught me good. I could work any sawmill I want."

He let the silence run for a long time, then got up and backed off the porch.

"I got plans," he said. He sat back down.

He followed her brown, unsettled eyes to the broken pattern of dry stalks in the empty field beside the Willard house, and to the bending sky that met the treeline above the river in a wave of pink light. He looked where she looked, at the perpendicular of the board fence that marked the small patch that was her family's front yard, and at the squared corners of a neighbour's house and at their woodshed and barn.

"Straight lines in a world God meant for crooked," Jane said.

"Straight trees," Jimmy said. "Straight cuts coming off the saw blade."

"It makes me wonder," she said.

"I wonder too. Not about straight and crooked. I wonder about how we start going one way, then start going another. Get turned around."

"Where were you going?"

He pointed to the setting sun. "I know a place. It's out west. Old Horsnell told me about it. He said it was where the woods play out to flat, open land. He said the wind was steady like breathing. Unfenced land running on forever. The kind of place where a man and woman could leave their mark. Make something of their lives."

He swung his shoulders to face Jane. For the first time their eyes met.

"I saved," he said. "I saved plenty for a start out there."

Again Jane looked over her shoulder and through the screened front door to her mother in the kitchen. Again he followed her eyes.

"We could go there if you want," he said.

Jane said nothing. Her eyes filled.

"We can tell your folks it was me." He reached his hand and touched her sleeve. "We can tell them together, tell them it was me."

CHAPTER 26

D elaney and Tom Johnson loaded a pushcart with hampers and bales of one thing or another. They leaned their shoulders into pushing it over the plank from the barge to the Yonge Street wharf. The load teetered. Johnson steadied it, and Delaney gave the cart his legs and back, breathing heavy. The cart hit the dock and jolted up Delaney's arms and across his shoulders. Johnson joined him behind the cart, and the two pushed it up the wharf to John Maher's Front Street warehouse. The entire time Delaney reached for his breath.

"Goods coming in," the warehouseman hollered from his makeshift pulpit at the centre of the long wooden building. He pointed to his left, to a long row of hampers, bales, and barrels.

Daylight filtered through sooty skylights.

Delaney and Johnson unloaded the cart and stacked the "goods coming in" onto eight-inch-high pallets. Delaney removed his cap to run a sleeve over his brow. He ran a hand through a headful of hair more grey than black.

"Goods going out," the warehouseman hollered, and pointed to his right.

Johnson snickered. "An echo he likes hearing. How many times a day, you think?"

"Sings it in his sleep," Delaney gasped, and put on his cap.

"To his wife," Johnson said. He pumped his hips. "Goods going in."

They pushed the cart across the warehouse and loaded it with "goods going out." A pasteboard sign identified the load as destined for the hold of the *Agnes Gretchen*, a two-mast schooner tied up at a nearby wharf.

As they were leaving the warehouse, Ben Geddes and Andy Stewart were pushing a load in.

"Last load," Geddes said to Johnson and Delaney.

Stewart hooted, "Cock-a-doodle-do."

The warehouseman hollered, "Goods coming in." He pointed to his left.

Johnson and Delaney delivered the goods to the *Agnes Gretchen* and returned the empty pushcart to Marr's Warehouse. They went to the warehouse office and reported their number of loads to a heavyset clerk who then signed them out.

They left the warehouse and entered a ramshackle shed with a few dozen clothes hooks on the walls and a round stone trough at the centre. Three hand pumps were evenly spaced around the trough. Delaney removed his shirt, revealing the wrinkle mass of burn scars on his chest and back. The palms and backs of his hands had scars as well. He hung the shirt on a hook. Johnson did the same. Delaney pumped water, and the two washed up. They changed into clothes that were not a whole lot better than those they had worked in.

Delaney checked his coat's breast pocket for the faded photograph of his family.

"You don't give up," Johnson said.

"It keeps me going," Delaney said.

They walked north on Front Street to the White Horse Tavern. It had a curved oak-panelled bar. Three bearded men sat at the bar staring into their whisky and beer. It was ten past quitting time, and already the sturdy oak chairs around a dozen or so tables were filling up with working stiffs taking their thirst seriously.

Delaney made the rounds, showing those he had not shown before the photograph and asking if they had seen any of his children. The answer was always the same, in as many ways as someone could say it — "No." He moved on to the Bull's Head and McCauley's taverns. He received the same response.

For the next two hours, he stood at the corner of Yonge and College and showed the photograph to passersby. He had been showing the photograph to anyone and everyone for the past four years, in taverns and on street corners, in Saint John, Montreal, and now Toronto.

Before sunset he started for his room above a green grocer in The Ward, a neighbourhood of thrown-together shacks with their insides spilling out. Along Terauley Street there were several torn wooden two-storey houses in danger of collapsing. Tarred poles braced against the walls and rammed into the rubble-strewn ground that held them up.

Dirty-face children in dirty clothes played in the street. Delaney looked at their faces. He looked at the faces of the people he passed. He recognized many of them. They wore the same long, hungry faces day after day. They wore deep lines and holes into their faces. They wore them down to nothing.

Through a ground-floor window, he saw an older woman, a grandmother, bathing a child in a wooden tub. The tub was on a table pulled to the window for the last bit of light. The glass was half-fogged from the hot water. The baby splashed with delight. The grandmother, in a wet grey smock, laughed at her unsuccessful attempts to scrub the child's face.

Delaney saw how the window light brushed gentle on the left side of the grandmother's face, and how shadow veiled her right side. The background fell off to darkness. Something about what he was seeing struck him as being true. The image seemed filled with unexplainable feeling, like the memory of his mother sinking a wooden scoop into a flour bin, or his wife lying in candlelight with rosary beads wrapped around her bloodless hands.

The grandmother looked up to see him. The smile disappeared. Through the glass she snapped, "Keep staring and you'll wear out your eyes."

He walked three more blocks to Albert Street and entered an alley that led to the back of a green grocer. He entered his room. He undressed in the dark and stretched out on the narrow cot propped against a wall. Sleep was hard to come by. Most nights he lay until the small hours listening beyond the darkness in his room, to the restless sounds of his neighbourhood.

On Sunday morning, he went to church, a different one each week, not to worship, but to stand outside and show the faithful his family photograph. At St. Michael's an attractive, well-to-do woman in a velvet coat and cape stopped to have a look. She had layers of brown hair with a small boat-shaped, lace-trimmed hat on top. She took the photograph from his hand and examined it.

He waited respectfully, a quiet-looking man, neatly dressed. White shirt yellow with age, collar not starched, and his dark wool trousers shiny at the knees and worn through where the cuffs broke over his scuffed and cracked black boots. He knew what some of the better sort would call him: "a shit shoe," a "shine rag." But not her. He could tell that when she looked at him. Kind eyes sparked with curiosity.

"Who was the photographer?" she asked.

"Stayner," Delaney said. "Richard Stayner of Halifax."

"Halifax indeed," she said, and again examined the photograph. "How long ago did your family pose for this?"

"Past twelve years."

"Hmm. And these are your children?"

"Yes."

"Hmm. How long have you been showing it to people?"

"For a long time."

"And no one has recognized them?"

He shook his head.

"I am not surprised. I hardly think they still look anything like this. The boy perhaps, not the girls. Even the youngest has become a woman."

She handed him the photograph.

"Portraits are so practised," she said, waving her hand as though shooing portraits from her mind. Her thin face tightened in displeasure. "They are so unnatural. For good reason, I know, but . . . well . . . I am a photographer. My views capture the dynamic of conflicting forces. The mechanical versus the human, the struggle . . ."

Delaney puzzled her words. He stepped aside for two gentlemen to pass.

"Where do you work?" she pressed.

"The waterfront, loading and unloading."

"And where do you live?"

"The Ward."

"You know the streets, I presume. The people there."

"I know the neighbourhood."

"And your children? How did you lose them?"

Delaney had looked away from her and at a young woman, with a baby on her lap, sitting on the top step of a brick house. He looked at the photographer and told her his story, which he had abbreviated to his wife dying, and him giving his children to a child and refuge home until he was better able to care for them, and that the home had bonded them into servitude, with no known whereabouts.

"Good Lord." She caught her breath and slowly released it. "How is that possible?"

Delaney shuffled in place.

"There must be something to be done," she said as she walked away. "There must be."

During the following week, Delaney heard that a policeman had made the rounds on the waterfront asking about him. From Dick Tobin, the warehouse manager, Delaney learned that a gentleman had made inquiries.

On Sunday he was outside St. Michael's showing church-goers his family photograph when the photographer woman approached him. She handed him a card and requested he come to her studio that afternoon at three o'clock, to meet her husband.

Delaney read the card. Her name was Frances Kennedy.

"I have a proposition for you," she said.

CHAPTER 27

O n Clinton Street, Delaney stood on the wooden sidewalk beside a gas lamppost, outside a red-brick, yellow-quoined, Victorian-style home. It had classic gables and a substantial front porch with intricate scroll-cut brackets connecting the posts. He admired the craftsmanship and enormity of the structure. A brass sign on one of the posts directed him to a side entrance, to the "Photography Studio."

Frances Kennedy welcomed him into the studio and offered him a chair while she called for her husband.

Framed photographs decorated the studio walls. Most of them "views" of the city. A parade of school children in coats and mufflers stomping their boots on the steps of Saint David's Church during a heavy snow. A concert band in a gazebo on the waterfront. A horse-drawn streetcar. The Yonge Street Arcade. A policeman standing under a gas lamp on Front Street and Wellington.

On the wall beside the open door to an office, which was dark with oak floor-to-ceiling bookcases, stood a mahogany cabinet with a glass door. Inside were various sizes of bottles and jars of powders and different-coloured liquids, each labelled in a careful hand: "Pyroxline," "Alcohol," "Ether," "Iodide of Potassium," "Silver Nitrate," "Cyanide of Potassium," "Hyposulphite of Soda." There was a large corked beaker that was labelled "Collodian."

Hanging above the cabinet was a gilt-framed photograph, a portrait of a man sitting on an armchair with a cushioned seat. Beside him was a lamp table with spindle-shaped legs and double crossbanding on the drawer front. There was a lamp on the table. Its light filled the right side of the man's face. Neatly cropped beard. Sharp nose. His left side was deep in shadow. The background was as dark as a root cellar. His expression was serious, intensified by the stark contrast of light and shadow. He wore a dark suit, a white shirt, and dark neckcloth.

Frances Kennedy returned and saw Delaney studying the portrait.

"Shadows provoke feelings," she said. "What do you see?"

"A man who shows off one side and hides behind the other."

"Well said." She held back a laugh.

A man entered the studio.

Delaney dropped his eyes. The man entering and the man in the portrait were one and the same.

"My husband," Frances Kennedy announced. She erupted in laughter.

Delaney squirmed.

The man held out his hand. "Eamon Kennedy."

⚓

Frances Kennedy's proposition was for Delaney to guide her through what she had called the "awkward sections of The Ward." In exchange, she and her husband would help him find his children.

The following day Frances Kennedy placed an etching of Delaney's family photograph in *The Globe*, accompanied by an advertisement calling for anyone who recognized the children Robina Delaney, James Delaney, and Annie Delaney should contact Eamon Kennedy. She promised to submit the advertisement every week, for as long as their arrangement was fruitful.

That first Saturday she photographed an overturned carriage on Yonge Street and a "view" of a horse-drawn streetcar passing the Shamrock Tobacco Shop.

"Not quite what I had in mind, Mister Delaney," she said, after developing the glass negatives. "They lack people. I want you to arrange photographs of people. Their situations. I want to reflect life in The Ward. I want my photographs to have feeling."

He thought about her request while at work and during his wakeful nights. He thought about people in their situations, stiff and staid in their sunlit poses. Sombre for the camera. Flat and unemotional. He thought about feelings in a photograph.

On Saturday morning he brought Kennedy to a stone yard where two men in leather aprons cut and shaped blocks of granite. A third man sat on a stool beside a granite slab, chisel in one hand, mallet in the other.

Kennedy looked the scene over. She pointed where she wanted Delaney to position the tripod and camera. The angle favoured the chiseller.

Kennedy looked through the lens. One man stood at a raw granite block with a sledgehammer, the other stood beside him with his hands on his hips. They both stared at the camera. She tilted the camera ever so slightly and took the photograph.

Before Delaney disassembled camera from tripod he sneaked a peek through the lens. The man with the sledgehammer and the one with his hands on his hips had walked away. But the chiseller still sat at the granite slab. Delaney suddenly saw what Kennedy had seen. In a shadow that fell across the chiselled granite slab, he read: "Ambrose Mader, b. August 2, 1838, d. May 4, 1878."

On another Sunday, he guided her to the back of a row house on Terauley Street. Broken boxes and crates and weathered boards thrown just anywhere cluttered the yard. Beside the backdoor was a pushcart with sacks of coal stacked on it. Kennedy stopped and gestured to a lit window. Inside a young man sat at a table with his hands held out and spread apart. A young woman sat before him. She was winding yarn around his hands. The couple were laughing.

Delaney set the camera on the tripod and loaded the camera with a glass negative. Kennedy eyed the scene and clicked the shutter button.

Outside Michael's Butcher Shop on Terauley Street, they captured a knife sharpener pumping water over his spinning stone, sizzling an edge on a long, straight blade. He was an old man with rounded shoulders draped in a dark frock coat. He had a straight nose as pointed as any knife he honed.

An hour before dusk they were on the waterfront where the *Lady Wellington*, a steam-driven sidewheeler, was moored at a jetty. Steam belched from two black funnels with three white bars painted near the tops. The steam cloud drifted over the deck and gave the ship an eerie appearance.

Delaney set tripod and camera at the stern. He angled it to see the full length of the ship. Kennedy slid behind the camera and pressed her eye to the lens. She drew away and looked at Delaney. Curious. Puzzled. She returned to the camera.

Delaney cupped his hands at his mouth and called out to anyone on board. "Hello, *Lady Wellington*."

A bearded sailor hung over the side.

Delaney called up to him. "Where you sailing?"

The sailor hung farther over the side and hollered down, "Buffalo."

Kennedy snapped the photograph.

ఆరి

For the next four weeks, photography was the only thing Delaney could think about. He saw photographs wherever he looked. Rain and gutter water gathering in wheel ruts. Darkened cobblestones. Slick wooden sidewalks in the glow from street lamps. Tom Johnson breaking into sunlight from the dark of the warehouse, his shoulders globed over the pushcart. Fresh blueberries in a woven basket.

On their fifth "photographic jaunt," as her husband called them, Delaney guided Frances Kennedy down Terauley Street past a jungle of shacks and dilapidated row houses. He pointed to rickety outdoor stairs that climbed to the upper floors, and to clothes-hanging poles poked out over the mud and cobble street. She said something to him, but her voice was lost in the tumult of rumbles and shouts and the clatter and clop of horse and carriages, pushcarts, and people.

They passed an old man with a white beard and rheumy eyes. The old man shooed them with a grumble and a sharp stone.

A bruiser, with a misshaped face shot red from drink, pulled his cap down and fell back against a wall. He grabbed at his crotch.

Kennedy looked away. The bruiser barked something lewd at her, then pulled a jar from his hip pocket and took a drink.

They passed a tavern with no name. They passed a betting shop where two men in soft caps and canvas pants were outside arguing. They passed a storage shed and a cobbler's shop with

156

a bench out front, passed Blind Turner the beggar and Bobbin' Charlie the match and bootlace seller. They passed a young girl sitting cross-legged on the wooden sidewalk selling weeds and dead branches and arguing both sides of a conversation.

Delaney said "hello" to her, but she offered no response.

"Do you know her?" Kennedy asked.

"Not her name," he said.

They turned down a narrow side street. It led into a maze of twisting alleys, some darker than others. Tucked between two tenements were a rag-wrapped mother and four scrawny kids. They sat around a firepit, which they had dug into the dirt and defined by cobblestones scavenged from a street.

Delaney set the box down and the tripod in place and took the camera from Kennedy and attached it to the tripod.

"We'll need more light," she said.

Delaney nodded. From a satchel hanging from one shoulder, he pulled a wrapped parcel and handed it to the woman. She opened it and grinned at the large cut of meat.

"Nothing posed," Kennedy insisted.

Delaney chuckled at how many times over the past few weeks she had cautioned him that a photograph should not be posed. At least it should not seem to be posed.

Delaney stoked the fire in the firepit. The mother set a pot of water on the grate and dropped the meat into it. Delaney told the mother to gather her children close to her.

Kennedy stepped behind the camera and focused the lens.

The fire blazed. The pot boiled. Steam rose before the faces of the family.

Kennedy clicked the shutter and stepped back from the camera, smiling at what she had seen through the lens.

Delaney thanked the woman and her children. He dismantled the camera from the tripod. He passed Kennedy the camera. "Another view?"

"So long as it works to our benefit," she said. She smiled.

Delaney led her across a footbridge over a narrow ditch, which heaved with the effluent from six open-door privies on its bank.

"Spice Island," Delaney said.

The privies looked onto a weed field of thistle and tansy. In the centre of the field, with the sun at her back, a woman sat on a three-legged stool. She was feeding gulls, dozens of them, with chewed and soggy bits of bread. The birds flew up when she tossed a morsel, then descended and fought for the little bit she had thrown.

Beyond the field, the sun gleamed off the copper dome of the Lunatic Asylum. In the opposite direction was the copper-clad spire of a Catholic Church.

The woman's stern face was thick with veins, her eyes empty.

Delaney mounted the camera on the tripod. From his shoulder satchel he took out a brown cloth bag. It was filled with bread crusts.

"This is for you, Mary Webb," he said. "There's a coin on the bottom. Don't throw that to the birds."

Kennedy loaded the camera with a glass plate and viewed the scene through the lens.

Mary Webb scattered a handful of bread for the birds. They flew down and flocked around her, screeching, fighting. She threw another handful. The gulls rose up, flapping wildly.

⚮

The darkroom had been converted from a large, walk-in closet. Kennedy entered it to develop the glass negatives and transfer the images to cardboard-backed paper. Delaney sat in the studio, on a wooden chair with floral paintings on the splat and rail. He saw two newly framed photographs on a wall. He remembered the taking of them both.

One was of a locomotive engine belching smoke from its stack and blasting steam from above the wheels. Through the steam and in the shadows were two horses rearing up at the engine. The other framed photograph was of a young woman with a babe in her arms, standing at an outdoor pump, washing clothes in a wooden trough. Looking at the camera. Fear in her eyes.

Delaney fell asleep in the chair and woke when Kennedy emerged from the darkroom. She had two photographs in hand and showed him one at a time.

The first was of the family that lived between two tenements. In the light flaring through the steam rising from the pot of boiling water, the family appeared almost dream-like. The background had gone black, as though the family were crouched at the fire before the mouth of a dark cave.

The second photograph was of the old woman feeding the birds on "Spice Island." With the sun at her back, she sat in a halo of light. Her face was sunken and starved. She looked as though she would be better served feeding the bread to herself than to the birds. Yet she flung the bread to them freely. Expressionless as the birds flew upward. A corpse among a flock of angels.

"I am well pleased, Mister Delaney," Kennedy said. "That saddens me."

Delaney was perplexed.

She took a deep breath. "I believe the arrangement we have is about to end."

Delaney was even more perplexed.

"This entire day I withheld information from you. I did so selfishly. I wanted the arrangement to continue." She went to the open door to her husband's study. "Eamon will explain." She gestured for Delaney to follow her in.

From the very first time he had seen through the open door into Eamon Kennedy's study, the wall-to-ceiling bookcases had intrigued him. The panoply of books had made an indelible impression. He had wanted to enter the study and touch them and read their spines. To do so would have violated the trust Frances had placed in him.

Now he stood inside the office surrounded by a world of learning. An eleven-volume set caught his eye. Gilt-edged and gilt lettering on the spine: *The Works of Ralph Waldo Emerson.* The first was titled *Society and Solitude.*

Eamon Kennedy, impeccably dressed in waistcoat and cravat, sat behind a mahogany desk reading a newspaper and smoking a meerschaum pipe with a face carved into the bowl. He got up and rounded a marble pedestal, with a bronze sculpture of a heron in flight. He suggested Delaney take the square-back armchair beside Frances. He got up and sat on the edge of the desk.

"Yesterday I received a letter from a law firm in New Brunswick," he said. "A response to the advertisement Frances placed with the newspaper. The firm has a signed affidavit from Simon Booth."

Delaney turned to Frances. Confused. Troubled. She looked at him apologetically.

Eamon Kennedy continued. "Simon Booth was the boss of a New Brunswick logging camp near the Miramichi River. He claims not long ago James Delaney worked in that camp."

Kennedy held up the affidavit. His voice softened. His eyes twinkled. "Simon Booth requests payment of the one hundred dollar reward my wife so generously offered, and I will so willingly pay. May good luck rise with you, Mister Delaney. And may you find your son."

"Shadows provoke feelings," Delaney said to Tom Johnson the following morning. Delaney had cashed in his pay slip and folded the money into his hip pocket. They walked from the warehouse office to a bollard on the wharf. Johnson sat, Delaney stood.

"What are you talking about?"

"Just something I learned," Delaney said. "Looking is not enough. Seeing is what it's all about. Seeing what's outside the light."

He held out his hand and Johnson stood to shake it.

"You don't know where he is, do you?" Johnson said. "Not for sure."

Delaney shook his head. "Logging camps and sawmills. In the letter he wrote, Simon Booth said that's where I should look for my son."

CHAPTER 28

A nnie stared from the kitchen window, her narrow face frozen behind the frozen glass. She watched Midwife carrying a lantern and cauldron of hot, bloody water across the yard, emptying it to punch a bloody hole into the snow piled against the barn. Her right hand prayed the stitches in the collar of her nightdress. Her left hand felt an emptiness through its cotton folds. She lifted her dark eyes to the fire on the hilltop. She heard his shovel in the frozen earth. The grieving sound turned her eyes to the rail fence poking through the sheeted snow, following it past a birch grove to where the moonlit river was like a curved blade stabbed into the heart of winter.

Midwife returned to the kitchen, holding up the lantern and shooing the shadows into the dark corners. The kitchen was sparsely furnished with a daybed, a pantry cupboard, and a deal table. Scattered about were four chairs with fancy scrollwork of bows and poppies. Midwife set her heavy self into one of these chairs set before a black iron stove. From a wooden tub she pulled out blood-stained swaddling and burned it in the stove. She poked up the coals and stared at them. She too could hear his digging. She also heard a stirring among the shadows by the window. She strained to see beyond the edge of lantern and stove light. "Annie?"

Annie's small voice squeezed forward. "You think burning and burying will make it go away. Nothing will!"

"What are you doing out of bed?" Midwife was on her feet and at Annie's side.

"But there was nothing I could do," Annie grieved. She choked back a hurt that clawed inside.

"No one could," Midwife consoled. "Sometimes it's just the way things are."

Annie looked past Midwife into the shadows, as though looking for something that was hiding in her mind. "You took him away and I never saw his face."

"It's better that way."

Annie's eyes were suddenly restless around the room. They settled on Midwife. "I have nothing to remember him by." She turned to the window to look at the fire on the hill.

Midwife saw the fresh blood on the back of Annie's dress. "Oh Lord you're bleeding again. Back to bed. Get your strength."

Annie's eyes shot up the stairs and widened. "Not up there! I won't go back to that bed."

"Here." Midwife took Annie's arm and led her across the kitchen to the daybed. "One of my girls will stay and do the lifting until you heal."

"I won't heal!" Annie gripped her sorrow and held it tight.

"You'll heal. We all do." Midwife's voice combed through Annie's flayed feelings. "You'll have another. You'll see. Hurt will sugar down to sweet."

"What sweet to hear him digging? Digging! What kind of husband is he?"

Midwife pulled a bolster under Annie's chin. "A time like this, digging and chopping is what a man does. It's how he straightens what he feels."

"What straightens it for me?"

"The loss. The beauty of it, knowing what lived in you was yours."

"Then it was not for him to choose!"

Midwife fixed Annie firmly and stroked her cheek. "God did the choosing, not him."

Annie pinched back a sob and closed her eyes.

"God has His own way of balancing things," Midwife said. "None of us can answer for that. Some days what God does cuts us to the bone, Annie. And some days God's doing is pure joy."

"I won't wait for God to do His doing."

"Don't talk such! God will turn it your way soon enough. Now lie still."

Annie drifted off for a moment, then came back. Her voice was swimming. "The things we know and don't know. The things we do. The things we should've done and didn't. I should've waited to marry Forrester. Mrs. Williamson said eighteen was old enough."

"More than old enough for child-bearing."

"I should've waited."

"Regret won't make up for the past." Midwife returned to the stove to finish the burning. "We bear what burdens us. Over time it lightens."

Midwife lifted a stove lid and stirred up the coals around the swaddling. Light swelled into the kitchen.

Annie turned to face the wall. "You don't know what's between us. I know what he's thinking out there. You heard him at the door complain. No name to carve. No name."

Midwife sneaked her eyes to Annie. "One will come. You'll see."

Annie turned from the wall to face Midwife. She sat upright and drew a shadow over her shoulders like a shawl. Her voice lowered to a bitter whisper. "I won't name it. A name would only make it worse."

"You're talking through your grief, Annie Forrester. It's not just mother-love that's grieving. You think he ain't?"

"He don't know how. I heard him. Knocking on his boots, sharpening the shovel to dig out there with his own hands."

"Who else is better than him to dig what needs digging? Digging out what's deep inside."

"Then he should dig it wider!" Annie swung her feet to the floor and stood and started for the door, stopping suddenly and doubling in pain.

Midwife caught her before she fell and helped her back into bed. She cooed comfort to settle her. "Give it time, girl. Rest and give it time. You'll see."

Annie sunk into the feather tick, exhausted.

Midwife got fresh swaddling from the upstairs and packed it to stop the bleeding.

"Two that love can't live together with something between them," Midwife whispered. A sadness fell over her face. She lowered herself to Annie's side. She fell upon her skirts and sat in silence for the longest time. She heard Annie's breathing deepen into sleep. She changed the dressing and burned the soiled swaddling in the stove. She went to the kitchen window and looked through the frozen glass at the fire on the hill. She listened to him digging.

CHAPTER 29

Delaney took his bearings from the orange and red patch of maple overlooking the bend in the river. The old fellow in town had said the river narrowed about a mile beyond the bend. He said there would be a log bridge for Delaney to get across.

Delaney crossed the bridge and struck out along a mud and gravel road. Shadows stalked from where the white pine was thickest. Truth is in the shadows. That's what Frances Kennedy had told him before he had left Toronto. The light only shows us where to look, she had said.

He leaned on a fence corner. Wheezing. Catching his breath. Mumbling out loud about the light flickering and dimming these last four years. He looked back at the canopy of trees overhanging the road he had travelled. He saw a tunnel of shadows deepening the more he looked, shadows breathing with the breeze.

They took a deep breath to hear him beg himself to stop and go no farther. Exhaled when he turned and stepped forward.

He walked until dark. He snapped pine boughs for a bed and star-counted himself to sleep.

A frost-heavy morning had him rubbing his legs awake and flapping the shivers from his body and bones. He coughed and gagged to clear his throat and lungs to breathe easier. From a shoulder pouch, he took a length of beef jerky and gnawed it while he walked.

The sawmill came up all of a sudden. It was a board building with two open ends. The mill wheel turned with the gush of water from a head pond backed up on the Pickerel River. There were three other buildings at the mill site: the mill office, a bunkhouse, and a cookhouse that had a sign over the door: "Eat And Get Out."

Delaney entered the mill office.

A man with a black, spade-shaped beard sat on a straight-back wooden chair. He bent over a split log for a desk, figuring a column of numbers on a sheet of foolscap. The split log had been nailed to two tree stumps that extended down through the floor and into the ground. The man looked up when Delaney walked in. He had laughing eyes and a set of broken teeth that showed through the whiskers.

"We don't have work if that's what you're looking for," the man said.

"Not for work," Delaney said. "I'm looking for a saw filer named Jimmy Delaney."

"No Jimmy here," the bearded man said. He got up with a blue enamel mug in his hand and went to a cylinder stove with a teapot on top. As he poured himself a mug he said, "I got an I-talian who does the filing here. He files real good."

"Did you ever hear of Jimmy Delaney?"

The bearded man sipped his tea and shook his head. "Not around here, and I know all the filers on Georgian Bay and the feeders into it. You want tea?"

"I would."

The man reached for another blue enamel mug on a slab-wood shelf. He filled the mug and passed it to Delaney. "What made you think he was here?"

"I've been asking at every sawmill and logging camp I can find," Delaney said.

The man pulled at his beard and sat down. He gestured to a slab-wood bench for Delaney to do the same. "That's one hell of a lot of sawmills and camps," he said. "There must be hundreds of them, more if you count the ones back east."

"That's where I started," Delaney said.

They both drank their tea, and the man said, "We're a big country."

"Bigger the more I walk it," Delaney said.

"It would be that. What'd this Delaney do for you to walk this far?"

"He's my son."

Delaney looked into the mug.

"I've been searching a long time," Delaney said. "I heard he had worked a logging camp on the Miramachi. The camp boss, a fellow named Simon Booth, wrote me and said my Jimmy was a damn good filer and a damn good man. He said Jimmy almost got himself killed saving another man's life."

Delaney paused and looked sheepishly at the bearded man. "Not my place to brag, is it?"

The bearded man shrugged. "I don't know whose place it should be. Where you going next?"

"Sawmill, logging camp. Village, town." Delaney's body sank into the wooden bench. "I have two girls I'm looking for too. Robina and Annie. I have no idea. None."

The bearded man finished his tea. Delaney finished his.

"There's a lumber barge at the mouth of French River," the bearded man said. "It sails the bay to Midland City. A rail line runs to Barrie. My name's O'Hara. Use it as far as it gets you."

CHAPTER 30

⤬

“I don’t know about this,” Robina appealed. She opened the door a little wider.

Mrs. Prichard’s lantern light sneaked through the darkness of Robina’s narrow room. It showed up a two-drawer dresser, a stool, and a rope bed with a straw tick. Open candles were not allowed in Prichard’s House, and lamp oil cost more than “the milk of human kindness.”

“They ask questions. You give answers,” Mrs. Prichard ordered. Her voice was vinegar and her mood a criss-cross of old-woman jealousy and bone-dry discontent. “The other girls already done it.”

“What questions?”

“None that’s hard to answer. There’s no right or wrong.”

“I’m not answering questions.” The young woman coiled from the doorway.

Mrs. Prichard bristled. “You don’t answer his questions and he could bring the police to this house. So you answer, or I send you back to those soldier boys to use you better than they already done. I don't much care what happens to you, but I don't want no police chief demanding more than I already pay."

Robina descended the dark stairs. In darkness she stood outside the closed door to the parlour. She worried more about the answers she would give than the questions that would be asked. She worried her voice would fail the way it had failed when Sheriff Green had asked, "Was he after Annie? Was that why?"

She had other thoughts that hobbled her outside the parlour door. She swallowed hard and entered the nest of shadows that were coiling and uncoiling in the corners of the room. A young man sat close to the room's only source of light, a tin oil lamp with a punched pattern of diagonal lines. The lamp sat on a spindle table that was wiggly from loose joinery. The faded blue-and-yellow-flowered wallpaper had peeled in places to reveal splotches of brown-painted plaster. Uncovered floorboards absorbed what little light spilled off the table or ricocheted off the walls.

No smile from the young man, just an abrupt nod that was all business. Yet, when he spoke, his soft voice seemed to curry the starchiness from his manner.

"My name is Woodward. I am an enumerator for the Federal Census."

Robina nodded without comprehension. Her eyes absorbed the dusty room that was Mrs. Prichard's private sanctuary.

"Please have a seat."

Robina remained standing close to the door, which she had left ajar. The dim light cut diagonally across her face.

Woodward shrugged at her insistence to stand. "Do you know what the Federal Census is?"

Robina made a puss and folded her arms as though annoyed.

"The census gathers vital information on every person in the Dominion of Canada for this year, 1881," he explained.

"The questions are personal, but not too personal. At least I don't think they are."

From the spindle table he withdrew a stack of census forms with a blank one on top. He selected one of several sharpened pencils from the table and poised it above the form to write.

"Mrs. Prichard said your name is Robina Delaney, but I did not write it down until I confirmed it with you. Is that who you are? Is that your name?"

For a moment Robina retreated to that faraway place in the past where her mother was showing her children what she had written in the blank pages at the back of the family bible. The names of their grandparents — *James and Hanora Delaney, of Ennis, Ireland; Robert and Winifred Doyle, of Ennis, Ireland.* Beneath the grandparents' names, she had written her husband's name and her name and the date of their marriage: *Arthur Andrew Delaney and Mary Hope Doyle, 18 May 1850.* Beneath the marriage date, Mary Hope Doyle Delaney had also written the names of her and Arthur's three children and their dates of birth. *James — 17 April 1851, Robina — 31 March 1853, Annie — 21 September 1856.*

"Yes. That's who I am," she said. Her voice so low, Woodward had to lean forward to hear.

"And it is Robina Delaney?" he confirmed.

She nodded.

"And of course you are female." Woodward smiled and printed the letter "F" in the box beside Robina's name. "Are you married?"

The weight of a man on top. Heart to heart. His pounding, hers as quiet as stone. Cooking Dooley Smith's meals, laundering his clothes. Robbing her of female privacy. Destroying her youth. A bought and paid-for arrangement, but not a marriage.

"No."

"Divorced? Widowed?"

She shook her head.

"Then you are single."

But never alone, not then, not with Annie to protect. Not with his clinging stink and clawing eyes. Not with the hungry way she weakened him with desire. Fawning for her. Bending to her pride. And not now, not with the hurt of loss and the broken image, a photograph torn to pieces and scattered. Not with her emptiness that needs filling if only for a night, an hour, for however long it takes until she cannot stand the feel of another man's skin.

"Yes. Single."

"What is your relationship to Mrs. Prichard?" Woodward started to print what he expected the young woman would answer, but lifted his hand at her delayed response.

Robina stared at him as though seeing him through a skein of thin cloth. A mousy man aging himself with mutton chops. Boosting his nerve with official forms and sharpened pencils.

"She runs this place," Robina replied. Her voice found a confidence that the questions would not be as challenging as she had thought.

"A boarding house, that's what Mrs. Prichard said it was," Woodward confided. "She said all the girls were boarders. Lodger is the appropriate designation. Although I am allowed to use the term boarder. Which do you prefer to be called: lodger or boarder?"

Robina did not budge to the census taker's feigned accommodation. She stiffened and leaned back against the door jamb, hardening to the imposition. "Most don't care what I am."

"I don't understand."

Robina dropped her eyes. "Boarder is good enough. Write down 'boarder.'"

Woodward did just that, careful at forming each letter.

"What was your age on your last birthday?"

"My last birthday?"

"Yes."

"Twenty-eight."

"And where were you born? In what city and province? If not in Canada, then what city and country?"

She hummed a single note that seemed to rise from a vivid sense of having been a child in a workingman's cottage on Tulip Street in Dartmouth. The five of them cosy in four rooms. There was a deal table and five chairs crowded in the kitchen, and a well-crafted open cupboard holding tinware and blue-coloured dishes. There was a rocker, a daybed, and a pine sideboard. A brown carpet covered the wooden floor. She remembered a crucifix covered by a purple Lenten cloth, and strands of palm stuck behind it.

The adjoining room contained a feather bed that was wide enough to sleep three across. And three across was how her, James, and Annie slept.

She could hear their mother singing them to sleep, and their father, from the kitchen, adding his off-key voice on the chorus, which had the three of them laughing through the next verse.

"Nova Scotia," Robina answered.

"What city or town?"

"Dartmouth."

"And after that you resided where?"

Robina could almost feel Annie and Jimmy pressing her hand as they sat on the boot bench in that dark hallway of the orphanage. Their shy faces in a cocoon spun from their mother's love.

Robina lifted her eyes to the census taker. "An orphanage, a farm in Aylesford, Nova Scotia," Robina replied, and Woodward wrote it down.

"What year was that?"

Robina counted back in her head. "Eighteen sixty-three, I think."

"And the month?"

Robina shook her head. "It was springtime. The orchard was all pink and white."

"The orchard?"

Robina waved off his question and heaved a sigh for a tangled memory that seemed so long ago.

"Before Winnipeg, were there other places where you resided?"

Robina shook her head. She did not want to remember any more of the places that scalded her.

Woodward reached for another pencil. "What religion do you profess?"

"What?"

"What church do you attend? Anglican? Baptist?"

"My mother was Catholic. That was the church she took us to."

"And your father?"

"He never went to church. None of the men did. Haven't you asked enough questions?"

"Just a few more. If you're tired of standing . . ."

"I'm tired of questions. I'm tired of you prying where you don't belong. I'm tired of you making me think."

"But the rest are only about your work and your wages . . ."

"I ain't telling nothing about what I do." Robina turned toward the door. "I'm not answering no more questions!"

Feelings spawned behind her eyes closed to the unloved faces taking their turn with her. She heard his pencil tapping the census form. Tapping. Slowly tapping, like a wall clock ticking into a silence. Then his voice peeled through the shadows, cold and distant. Demanding.

"You have to answer. It's the law."

Robina shivered. She slowly turned back and slowly made her way to the chair opposite the census taker. She sat.

"Where was the law when I needed it?" Her soft voice slipped among the faded flowers in the wallpaper. "No one cared enough to ask questions then."

CHAPTER 31

D elaney lowered his end of a railway sleeper and set it in the gravel roadbed. He wheezed for breath.

Fergus O'Brian lowered his end. Young, smooth-shaved, brown hair to his shoulders, and built like a draft horse.

"How old are you anyway?" O'Brian teased.

"Old enough," Delaney said.

"To be Moses to my dad," O'Brian laughed.

With a story stick, he measured the sleeper's distance from the one beside it. He flipped the stick to Delaney and Delaney measured off his end of the sleeper.

They walked back along the gondola car of ballast, and several flatbed cars with enough sleepers and steel rails for the section gang to lay two miles of torn-up track. A freight car had jumped a rail. It had left behind a tangle of black sleepers and bent steel, which the section gang had cleared away.

They reached the flatbed and O'Brian dragged off a hemlock sleeper and lifted it to his shoulder.

"Take a rest, old man," he said. He carried the creosote sleeper and set it in place.

Delaney scooped water from a bucket and leaned against the steel knuckle that connected one railcar to another. Ten more ties, he figured. Another day's sweat and sore muscles.

O'Brian returned for another sleeper.

"Your old lungs still catching a breath," he joked.

Delaney stubbornly pulled forward a sleeper and shouldered it.

"Not on your own, old man," O'Brian said, and slipped under the sleeper to take most of the weight. "We drew lots for working with you. I lost."

Delaney chuckled and moved to one end of the sleeper.

After setting the last ten of them, they joined eighteen others at lugging one ton rails from a flatbed. They pry barred them onto the sleepers and spiked them down. By the time the section boss blew the whistle for the workday's end, Delaney was exhausted. His back ached, and his chest and grey head dripped sweat. He closed his eyes on the work train into town and sunk inside a sparkle of memories that sometimes lightened his load.

He imagined snow on a window ledge. The glass half-fogged on the inside. Mary with her pained face disguised by a smile, ironing clothes beside a cast-iron stove. A catch pot of stew at the back.

Robina in her mother's rocker. Her cheeks and forehead pale to the darkening of her hair and eyes. A ball of green yarn in her lap. Her knitting needles clicking out a scarf or tuque.

Annie on the floor at her mother's feet, her lips parted in a song. Her eyes glinting from the lantern light.

And Jimmy with his back against a wall, his jaw hardening

to a grumble of coming-of-age discontent, reluctantly making an arm muscle for his father to feel.

Delaney collected these memories in a black bound notebook. He spent his Sundays writing them down, what he called "the photographs in my mind." After eighteen years of searching, he now believed the family photograph and his memories were the closest he would ever come to being with his children. This anguish stuck to him like a cobweb.

One Sunday night, he strained against the strength of the dead in that Confederate prison shadowing the faces of his children and that of his wife. He sat weeping at a wobbly table, staring at the notebook. He heard a knock. With lantern in hand, he went to the door and listened. Someone moaned on the other side.

That low sound of pain and fear and unhappiness became a handhold for him to climb from his own grief. He opened the door and lowered the lantern to see a woman huddled in his doorway. A brown shawl covered one side of her head. He drew back the shawl, and she grabbed his hand.

"I knew your door," she groaned. Her pale young face had been beaten black and blue, and her left eye was swollen shut. She smelled of whisky.

Delaney helped her to her feet and into his room. He set the lantern on the table and seated her in his only chair.

She looked up at him and, favouring the battered side of her face, offered him a thin smile.

"Been watching you," she said, her voice wilting. "Coming and going. We all been watching. We see how you are, how you are with people. I felt safe coming here."

On the table, beside the open notebook, was the photograph of his family. The woman brought it into the lantern light and cocked her head to see it with her unbruised eye. Gently she touched the faces of Robina and Annie, and then Jimmy and Mary.

Delaney had a pot of tea on a small coal burner. He poured a cup and placed it on the table.

She held the photograph in one hand and splayed her other hand over the open page in the notebook. She drew the photograph to her breast and lowered her head. After mumbling something to herself, she laid the photograph beside the notebook.

"Most of us don't pick the life we get," she said, and reached for the tea with both hands and drank it.

He gave her his cot in a corner of the room. He curled up behind the coal burner. In the morning, he laid out bread and tea for her and left for work. When he returned to his room that evening, she was gone.

Twice, as he walked to and from the platform where he caught the work train, he saw her outside McNulty's Tavern. He nodded to her, but she did not nod back.

A few weeks later, the section gang travelled a hundred miles into the bush to lay track to a nickel mine near Sudbury. Woodsmen cut fir trees for the cookhouse to burn. They strategically piled slash near the work gangs and burned it for the smoke to drive off swarming blackflies.

Delaney coughed at the smoke filling his lungs, the way it had in that Aylesford farmhouse so many years ago. Fire running up his back. Holding his coat closed over the two little girls, and the fire burning down his arms and melting his hands into rope-like scars.

He coughed hard and stepped away from the burning piles of slash. Through the drifting smoke, he watched a wheel of men driving spikes into rail plates. His mind framed the spike drivers with smoke drifting in the foreground and slash piles hellishly burning behind.

After the gang had laid nearly twelve miles of track, it started to rain. It rained heavy for two days. The downpour turned the track bed and hillside to treacle.

The gang waited out the rain in the travelling bunkhouse. Delaney sat on a bottom bunk listening to the younger men gab about everything and about nothing at all. Suddenly, his ears perked to hear Duncan Boise tell Fergus O'Brian about a pretty friend of his wife's named Annie Delaney. Delaney trembled at Boise saying that name. He got up and stood beside the two men. He asked Duncan Boise to repeat the name he had just said.

"Annie Delaney," Boise said. "Though it could be anything now. Pretty girl, like as not married that farmer named Forrester."

"Where was that?" Delaney asked.

"Where I'm from," Boise said. "Smiths Falls. It's near Ottawa."

CHAPTER 32

The minister's son led Delaney from the white clapboard Anglican Church in Smiths Falls and down the tree-lined road. The maples had lost their colour, and the rolling farmland was an unblemished wrapper of brown stubble.

"My father says the Lord saves those who are crushed in spirit," the fourteen-year-old said.

Delaney kicked through brown leaves, which had blown over the road.

"The Lord will wipe every tear from our eyes," the boy insisted.

Delaney nodded unconvincingly.

Less than a mile outside of town, the boy pointed to the weathered farmhouse set before a grove of white birch. Smoke rose from the chimney.

"He stopped coming to church," the boy said. "He seldom comes to town."

Delaney thanked the boy and walked down the gravel wagon path to the house. His step was slow, his face anxious.

Boards covered the second-floor windows of the two-storey wood-frame house. Grass grew up to the first-floor windowsills. Dried apples covered the ground. Five red hens ranged in the farmyard and in a plot that had once been a vegetable garden. Through the open barn doors, Delaney saw a farm wagon and a carriage. Beside the barn were a harrow and a hay rake. High grass grew over them.

He climbed two steps to the stoop. In the kitchen window stood a tall, starched man staring out beyond the barn. He made no sign of seeing Delaney on the stoop. The man was Michael Forrester.

Delaney knocked. Forrester did not answer. Delaney entered. Forrester turned from the window.

"She said you would come," Forrester said. "Some woman told her you were dead, but she refused to believe it. For years she waited for you to come."

Delaney wondered how Forrester knew who he was.

Forrester sat in a stuffed chair beside the stove.

"Once she brought home a young sparrow with its tail just budding," Forrester said. "It could not feed itself, so we made pills of food, and Annie coaxed them down its throat."

He gestured for Delaney to sit in the wooden chair at the table.

"She was kind like that," he said. "I didn't know it when she was here. Paid no attention. I don't even know if what I remember was real."

Delaney sat before a blue-flowered porcelain place setting. On the other side of the table was a chipped brown mug.

Forrester crossed and uncrossed his legs. "We weren't married long," he said. "She worked in the dry goods store, and I bought more of what I didn't need. A lot of what I didn't want. Just to go in. She was so pretty."

Delaney remembered Annie's bobbed hair and busy eyes. He remembered her tiny voice asking, "Where?"

"To Babylon," he had answered, unable at that moment to think of what else to tell her. He had gathered her into his arms. "Mama went to Babylon."

Annie had smiled brightly and wiggled free. "How many miles to Babylon? Three score miles and ten. Will she get there by candlelight?"

Delaney had chimed, "Oh yes, and back again."

He looked off Forrester and blinked back a feeling.

"She had other suitors," Forrester said. "Half a dozen maybe. She said I reminded her of you, but I don't see how. In what way do you think she meant?"

Delaney shook his head. "I don't know how much she would remember about me."

Forrester started to say something but stopped. He looked out the kitchen window. He looked at Delaney. "I don't know how she knew you would come."

Delaney thought about it. He lowered his eyes to the blue-flowered plate, teacup, and saucer. He realized he was sitting in Annie's seat.

"I gave up looking three years ago," he confessed. "I couldn't go on. Year after year, getting nowhere."

He touched the rim of the blue-flowered plate. "I lost hope," he said. "The years emptied me out."

Forrester got up and went to a pine hutch for a framed photograph. He stood at the table and handed it to Delaney. It was a photograph of Annie in a fancy dress and Forrester in an oversize frock coat.

Delaney remembered showing Mary and their children their family photograph, and how they had stared at it, awed at seeing themselves caught in a gesture that seemed both odd and familiar at once. Mary had remarked how close Annie resembled her as a little girl and how much Jimmy and Robina looked like him. Mary had started to say something else, but a choke of pain trapped the words in her mouth. He had gathered her in his arms and held her close. When her pain subsided, she had pointed at the photograph and pulled his hand to her heart. "Promise me, Arthur, promise you'll keep it like this, keep them together, a family."

Delaney reached back the photograph, but Forrester waved it off.

"You keep it," Forrester said and sat in the chair before the chipped brown mug.

Delaney got up and returned the photograph to the hutch. "Some things help us remember," he said.

Forrester gripped the edge of the table. "I got my share of them in this kitchen." He nodded to the stuffed chair. "It's where she sat, looking out."

Delaney was standing beside the stuffed chair. He looked out the window. It framed a hilltop on which there were two wooden crosses.

"We had sheep for awhile," Forrester was saying. "A ewe was lambing, and the lamb was coming breech. I was awkward about it. Unable. Scared. She got down and inserted her hand and cupped a fetlock and manoeuvred the leg for birthing. The other leg too. Then she got hold of the legs and pulled and the lamb slid out and when it baaed her face lit up." He started to cry, then abruptly stopped. "You'll want to go up there, won't you?"

Their eyes met.

"I would," Delaney said. He started to say something else, but his voice caught and he looked away.

"I won't go there," Forrester said. "I can't."

"I understand," Delaney said. He got up and touched Forrester's arm.

"No, you don't understand." Forrester trembled. "Midwife said I should. She said it was the religious thing to do. She said Annie would have wanted it. But I couldn't."

He got up and went to the window. His voice was thin like smoke. "I dug my son's grave, but I could not dig hers."

CHAPTER 33

An old beggar sat in the dirt in light from the front window of Jugg's Saloon on Cassidy Street, the main street in the town. He looked up at Delaney.

In his blazing eyes Delaney saw madness like that of soldiers in the dark cellar of that prison camp. The beggar's voice had a disconnected tone, as though he were mouthing words running wild in his mind.

"A blood river," the beggar said. "And canyons and kingdom come scoured of its secrets." He held out his open hand to Delaney.

Delaney dug a penny from a pocket and gave it to the beggar.

"The kind of secrets a woman keeps to herself," the beggar said. "The kind it takes a crazy man to know."

The beggar removed a ragged red cloth from around his neck. He pointed to the thick scar.

"The mark of Cain," he said, and laughed and folded over into a heap of rags.

Delaney walked through the splay of evening shadows in the town. He walked toward firelight spilling from the open double doors of a blacksmith's stable. He wheezed in a breath and leaned his tired body against the jamb.

The blacksmith pumped the bellows. His eyes gleamed and his cheeks reddened from the hissing coals. With his forearm, he wiped sweat from his brow and from his close-cropped dark hair. He trimmed the coals with a poker and pumped the wooden shaft. The coals whitened and a few shattered in their own heat. He held the wooden shaft on his shoulder. He looked at Delaney.

"Jimmy Delaney," Delaney said.

The blacksmith raised the shaft. With metal tongs, he lifted a length of bar iron and set it among the glowing coals. He crossed his arms at his chest. "His farm is a long way from here. You walking?"

Delaney nodded.

The blacksmith removed a potato from a warming grate above the coals and tossed it to Delaney. "Walking will be dry and hot this time of year."

Delaney cooled the potato with his breath and ate it.

"You look worn," the blacksmith said. "It could take you forever."

Delaney smiled. "How far is forever?"

The blacksmith dug the bar deeper into the coals. "A day's walk to the crossroads, then a half-day beyond that. You know Jimmy Delaney, do you?"

"He's my son."

"Well I'll be." The blacksmith smiled. "A rest will do you good. There's an empty stall out back."

Delaney removed his brown slouch hat. He unslung his canvas pack and laid out his bedroll. He used a leather harness for a pillow. He listened to the blacksmith hammering, to a horse snorting and breathing in the stall beside him, to a buckboard passing, to distant voices that took him far away to his home near the shipyard in Dartmouth where he flat-ironed his wife's best brown dress, the one with the lace on the collar and cuffs, the one he had buried her in.

❧

He woke before midnight and slung his pack and bedroll over his shoulder. The blacksmith lay awake on a cot beside the furnace. He nodded to Delaney and Delaney nodded back.

He walked the dusty road all night, with enough moon and stars to light his way. A keen wind blew cool and dry, and on it came the smell of sage and of the ground giving up its warmth. At the crossroads, he rested against the bank of a gully and ate beef jerky and hardtack. The sun came up. Not far away, beside a dry creek bed, he saw a cone-shaped hut and two people standing outside it.

He rested for more than an hour, then climbed from the gully and turned to get his bearings. For a moment, he lost his sense of direction to the high, cloudless sky and the vastness of the landscape. As though framing a scene through a camera, he cupped his hand around his right eye to stop it from seeing beyond what his mind could comprehend. The sun spread long and even over the dirt and stone and dry stalks. To him, it was like a brown, windswept ocean that sailed on forever.

He filled a pipe and smoked it as he walked. A doctor had told him smoking would ease the huskiness in his lungs and throat. Before long he stopped to wet his lips from a leather canteen and blow dust cake from his nose. He could see a farmhouse tucked this side of a windbreak of trees.

An hour later, he recognized the new wood framing of a barn being built and men lumbering wood from a skidway of logs. He wondered which of those men was Jimmy. He wondered whether he would recognize his son without being told, and whether his son would recognize him. And he wondered what he would say to Jimmy when they met, and what Jimmy would say to him.

CHAPTER 34

J ane came from the house, with a child on her hip and carrying a pail of water. She carried child and pail to the skidway. The lanky man with the round black hat, which he cinched under his chin, called out, "Someone's coming." Jane looked to where he pointed to the road that led from town.

The other men all strained to see what he saw. One of the men guessed at who the man on the road was. The others just watched the growing speck of someone heading their way. One of them hollered into the barn that a stranger was coming.

As the men gathered round and dipped for water, Jane asked, "Anyone know that walk?"

The men looked harder, shrugged, and shook their heads. All were curious that someone whose walk they did not know was this far from town.

"There's something about it," Jane said. "The way he holds himself."

She carried pail and child into the post-and-beam barn. Late afternoon sunlight buttered the new wood framing. She set the child on the dirt floor and called into the rafters, "I have water."

Jimmy Delaney walked a beam to a ladder and climbed down. Their thirteen-year-old son followed him. He and Jimmy both wore bib overalls with mallets in the hammer loops. The boy had Jane's round face and dark eyes. Jimmy tousled the hair of the child on the floor, then dipped the ladle for water and passed it to the boy.

"He still can't keep up with his old man," he said to Jane, winking. He accepted the ladle back from his son and dipped for himself.

She smiled at the boy. "Don't mind him, Thomas. You will outwork him some day, and he knows it."

"It'll be a while before I slow down," Jimmy said, teasing her.

She teased right back, "But you will, and won't I be a woman blessed."

Jimmy dipped for another mouthful, then said, "Ted hollered that a stranger was coming."

"Walking from town it looks like," she said.

"How far away?"

"A half-hour, maybe."

Jimmy and Thomas went back into the rafters to continue souring the mortise and tenon joints with pine resin and linseed oil.

Jane returned to the house. From the kitchen window, she anxiously watched the man on the road walking. For a reason she could not figure, she felt change coming with each one of his steps.

ᔕᓂ

The men were back squaring logs and lumbering boards when Delaney turned off the road and walked the long wagon way toward the barn. He reached the skidway and pulled off his hat to a head full of grey hair. Dust and sweat caked his face. He had parched lips and wobbly legs and a tired croaky voice that said, "I'm looking for Jimmy Delaney."

The lanky man pointed to the barn. "Jimmy's in the rafters."

Delaney pawed his face. Those crowded around him saw the wrinkled mass of scars on his hands and on the left side of his neck. One of the men with no shirt looked past Delaney to the road and beyond that to the crossroads and beyond that to the town.

"Did you walk from town?" The man in bib overalls asked with an accent that sounded German.

"That's more than fifty miles," a man in a red shirt piped with doubt.

Delaney searched their faces before answering, "I walked a long way."

"How far?" the man in red chimed.

"A long way. Halifax. Dartmouth. I walked from Nova Scotia."

"You walked that far."

Delaney nodded. "Mostly. That's where I started."

"Christ damn!" the man in the round hat exclaimed, and others said something that also marvelled at the stranger walking what must be nearly three thousand miles.

"How long did it take?" The man with no shirt asked.

Delaney looked to the house, then down the road as though measuring the distance he had come and the time it had taken him to do it. "A long time," he said, more to himself than to the men. "Since 'sixty-seven."

The man in the round hat shouldered up. "That's over twenty years. You walked that long to see Jimmy Delaney?"

Delaney turned to him. "I did."

The man in the round hat shook his head. "It must be one hell of a goddamn important thing to walk that long and that far. What is it?"

Delaney dropped his eyes, as though he knew what he was about to answer would make no sense at all. "I want to tell him who I am. I want to tell him I'm sorry for what I did."

The man in the round hat pulled a puss. "You walked all that way?"

The man in the red shirt, which was now ablaze in the slanting sunlight, shouted over his shoulder into the rafters, "Hey Jimmy! Stranger out here walked a long time to tell you who he is."

Delaney heard someone inside the barn shout back, "Who?"

"He didn't say," the man in the red shirt hollered. "He wants to tell you who he is."

Through an unsheathed section of framing, Delaney angled to see Jimmy climb down from the rafters. A boy climbed down after him. The two emerged from inside the framing. Jimmy blinked in sunlight and shielded his brown eyes to get a good look at him. "How far did you say?" Jimmy asked and closed the distance to where the men were standing with their saws and chisels hanging dumbly at their sides.

Delaney saw the resemblance right off. From the way Jimmy looked at him, Delaney figured Jimmy did too. The two of them thick in the shoulders, full heads of hair, Delaney's grey and matted from his hat, Jimmy's shiny with sweat and blowing up brown waves in the breeze. They took a similar stance with arms folded at the chest and staring at each other, spellbound beneath the high sky in the yard between the framing of the new built barn and the farmhouse.

The screen door flapped open and flapped shut. Jane, still with the child on her hip, walked over to where her husband and Delaney stood.

The men elbowed closer to hear every word the two spoke.

Delaney said, "I feared I wouldn't recognize you, but there is no doubt. I have a photograph I kept looking at all these years. I gave you one. Do you remember?"

Jimmy dug his hands inside his bib overalls. He blinked several times, his mind seemingly lost in a memory.

"We were all together in this big room," Delaney said. "A pendulum wall clock and a table with clawed feet. Annie kept rubbing them."

Jimmy stared at him.

Delaney appealed to Jimmy's memory. "I gave each of you a photograph of all of us posed around your mother, just before she died. 'So you don't forget,' I said. All of us in the photograph, so you don't forget."

The woman, Jane, hitched up her child and curled an arm around her husband's waist. She studied Delaney as though trying to read meaning in what he had said.

Jimmy swallowed hard. His voice broke apart with feeling. "I remember a lot of things, old man. A lot of things. I remember the mother who gave me birth and the family I was born to. I remember her bed before the fire, and her face pinched with dying."

His face puckered. He looked at Delaney, whose cheeks were like wax melting off his jaw. Jimmy said, "I got a photograph in my head that helps me remember. That's all I got."

Delaney sunk into himself as Jimmy said, his voice as sour as the linseed and pine resin stink on his clothes. "I got no time for the dead come back to life. I got a barn to build."

Delaney buckled as Jimmy turned away and called the men back to work. Tears rolled down Delaney's cheeks. He reached for Jane's arm to steady himself.

"He's not like that," she consoled. "That's not like him. It's the short days."

She led Delaney to the house. "He's worried they won't finish the barn before the snow blows in."

Delaney lowered his pack and bedroll to an empty nail keg outside the front door. He sat on another one beside it.

He took a long look around at the fresh wood of the barn. It shamed the battered boards of the old barn and storage shed. Lined against the front wall of the house were several stone crocks and wooden barrels and buckets. Near the door was a wooden butter churn. He looked across the field of dry stalks and across another field that had been recently manured.

"This all his?" he asked.

"Ours," Jane corrected. "Mine and Jimmy's, and two other families, the Hahns and the Bakers. We work it together." She gestured to the men at the skidway. "Ted Hahn is the one with no shirt. He and Greta live a mile up the road. And Gabby Baker, he's the one who could talk a priest out of church. Gabby and Jimmy go back to working the logging camps. Him and his wife, Katherine, live not far beyond Ted. The fellow in the red shirt is Augie Walker. He's a neighbour."

She opened the door and went inside. Delancy stayed sitting. The play of late afternoon light outside the barn caught his attention, the way it honeyed the fresh-cut boards and slanted through the upright posts, falling evenly over Jimmy Delaney and his son, the two of them hunched inside the framing and smearing a beam with pine resin.

Delaney knew Jimmy's gestures like they were his own; the angle at which Jimmy cocked his head when he concentrated on his work, the way Jimmy squared his shoulders, the way he held the brush and dipped it into the pine pot. If it wasn't for the barn, the dirt, and the openness of the countryside, he could have been looking at himself twenty-five years ago in the Dartmouth shipyard.

Just then Jimmy looked up at Delaney, held his eyes, and then quickly looked away.

Delaney sunk down to the bench and removed his thirsty boots.

"You coming?" Jane called.

Delaney got up and entered the house.

CHAPTER 35

The kitchen stove pumped out a heat that was dozy and dry, the kind of heat that eased the ache in Delaney's muscles and joints. The room smelled of roast pork. It was sparsely furnished with a long deal table, at which Jane stood with a jug, pouring out a mug of cider. A flour bin was tucked under the table. A pantry cupboard leaned against the wall opposite, filled with pickles and preserves. Beside it a pine food safe held dry goods. Scattered about were eight chairs. The child sat on the scrubbed wooden floor at Jane's feet and stared up at Delaney.

Delaney pulled a chair close and leaned over. "I had three of my own," he said.

"I know," Jane said. She passed him the mug of cider. "You're his father, aren't you?"

Delaney nodded.

She held out her right hand. "I'm Jane." Her smile filled her puckish cheeks and lit up her dark brown eyes.

Delaney smiled back. He shook her hand. "I'm Arthur Delaney." He patted the child's head. "I'm pleased to meet Jimmy's family."

She picked up the child and held him out as though to show him off.

"There's more," she said. "The oldest is with Jimmy, and Greta Hahn has Mary while we're building the barn."

Delaney sipped the cider and wiped his mouth with the back of his scarred hand.

Jane stared at Delaney. She said, "Jimmy Delaney is the kindest man I ever knew, but he won't talk, not about himself and not about his past. He said he had two sisters and he doesn't know where they are, and that he had a mother that died when he was ten. When he said nothing about his father, I knew there must have been trouble."

The child squirmed, and Jane set the child on the floor.

"Now I'm worried," she continued. "I'm more than worried, Arthur Delaney, I'm scared. I'm scared your coming could spark a change that I cannot control. My husband never once turned his back on anyone. He always had a kind word, an invite for supper, the offer to unroll a blanket in front of this stove. But he turned his back on you, his father. And now you're here in this kitchen, and I don't know what from what."

She got up and went to the door and looked out.

Delaney needled a finger into the child's belly and made it laugh. "What's his name?"

He looked at her framed in the doorway. The angled sun glanced off the side of her head and highlighted the straw-coloured hair.

"James, after his father. We call him Jimmy Boy. His sister's name is Mary, like Jimmy's mother. She's four. The oldest is Thomas, after my father. We sometimes call him Thomas Henry, the whole name just like that. Mostly when he's bad, which is not very often. He's thirteen."

She smiled sadly at a thought she had.

"And Henry?" Delaney asked.

"Henry?"

"You said you sometimes call him Thomas Henry."

Jane looked to one side to avoid his eyes. "Henry just came out of thin air."

Delaney crouched to scoop Jimmy Boy into his arms, but the child squealed, cried, and looked to his mother for help. Jane took Jimmy Boy into her arms and the child clung to her neck. She returned to the door and looked again at the men lumbering outside the barn. She faced Delaney. "Jimmy said the youngest was the one he worried about the most."

"Annie," Delaney said and reached into his coat pocket and withdrew the faded photograph.

She took the photograph. "Jimmy said they got separated and that he had tried but didn't know where to start looking. I think he blames himself for not knowing where they had gone."

Jane studied the photograph. "Jimmy said he had a photograph of his mother and sisters, but someone took it from him."

"I gave the same as this to each of them," Delaney said. "Buried one with their mother. I carried that to keep me going."

Jane sat with Jimmy Boy on her lap. "I want to know," she insisted. "I want to know it all."

Delaney nodded. "And I want to tell you. I need to tell you." He wheezed to catch his breath. He held up the empty mug.

"Of course," Jane said, embarrassed she had not offered. She filled the mug and passed it to him.

He drank and set the mug on the table. He leaned forward, hung his elbows over his knees, and rested his chin in his hands. "Mary and me were married thirteen years. Not long enough, not for our children. Not for me. The years you can't get back. The things you do. The way you fail. You want to know, I'll tell you. I made Mary a promise before she died. I failed to keep it."

CHAPTER 36

J immy and Thomas walked through the skeleton of a barn and out through the back to where Ted Hahn nailed battens over board seams. Jimmy waved his hand toward the land that slanted a quarter-mile down to a stream.

"Next year we'll build a windmill," he said to Thomas. "We'll pump water uphill to the house and barn. We'll build one for Gabby and one for Mister Hahn."

Thomas pointed to the house. "Who's that man?"

"He's a man who walked a long time to get here," Jimmy said. "He walked from a past I thought I forgot."

"I don't understand," Thomas said.

"I don't either."

Ted Hahn reached for another batten to nail over two boards. "Most of us travelled out here to forget about something," he said.

Jimmy breathed deeply and nodded. He turned from Hahn and Thomas and looked out past the stream. "I came here because

199

an old man put a dream in my head. It had never seemed real, something I could never do, until one day with Jane, sitting on her front porch, it was like I knew just where to go."

"We all came here for a dream, Jimmy," Hahn said.

Jimmy looked through the barn at the farmhouse. "This place turned out to be everything I dreamed it would be. A place so empty I could step outside myself and lose the past I didn't like. But it doesn't work that way, does it?"

"We can't help choosing the past we like best," Hahn said. "But sooner or later it all catches up." He dug a nail from the leather pouch that was strapped around his waist.

"Family wounds are the deep ones," he said. "Most don't heal on their own. And sometimes you got to salt them to get the healing started." He drove the nail into the batten, then said to Thomas, "Help me carry over some boards." The two walked off.

Jimmy leaned against a post and slid down to his haunches. He remembered the Children's Refuge and Aid Home and the dark front hallway within. He saw the big oak door closing him off from his father who was standing in the hallway, sad, bewildered. He had wanted to holler something through the closed door to his father, but was so tongue-tied with fear that he could not even whimper.

He got up and went to the house and sat on a nail keg outside the door. He heard Jane say something, then Delaney said, "Four years in a Confederate prison. I might as well have been dead. By the time I got home, she had bonded them out. There were no records for them after that."

He heard Jane say, "You've been looking for them ever since."

"All that time I ached to turn things right."

Jimmy wrapped his arms around himself. He looked at the reddening horizon and the three men stacking boards and storing tools in the old barn. He saw Thomas walking his way. He wiped his tears so his son would not see.

CHAPTER 37

Jimmy Boy squealed at a drowsy fly that had landed on its nose. Jane shooed it and turned back to Delaney. She waited for him to continue, but he was staring at the heavy iron pot on the back of the stove.

He turned and faced Jane. "I was scared of being a father without her. Running off to war was a coward's way out. I paid for it in that prison."

Jane hugged Jimmy Boy tight for the shame that had spread over Delaney's face. She saw a man weary from a long time on the road, a man stooped under his past.

"I'm not one to throw stones," she said. She set Jimmy Boy on the floor and opened the oven to a blast of heat. With a long fork she poked the pork roast. The juice ran pink. She closed the oven door and reached around the stove into a wood box for two sticks of wood that were as thick as her fist. She lifted a lid and fed the fire. Before closing the lid, she lit a taper and went to the table and struck a lamp.

"We all shamed ourselves at one time or another," she said, and waved out the taper.

She looked out the window at the low sun, at the windbreak of uneven branches, at the twisting stream bed, and at the perpendicular of the rail fence and the squared angles of the new barn.

"There was a time I wanted a world made straight," she said. "The crookedness of God's world troubled me. I know better now. There are no straight paths. We easily wander off and get ourselves lost. The lucky ones find their way again. I am one of the lucky ones."

She opened the door and called to Jimmy and Thomas that supper was ready. She turned to go back in when she saw them sitting on the nail kegs.

"I heard," Jimmy said to her.

"Everything?"

"Enough."

"Then you got thinking to do," she said.

Jane and Thomas went into the house.

❧

Jimmy walked to the new barn and stood in the centre of it. He looked out at the house and the sun setting behind it. The time it takes, he thought. The choices.

He walked from the barn to the stream and stood beside it watching eddies of water creaming in the last rays of sunlight. He turned back toward the house. He saw his father in the lit window looking out. Looking for him.

CHAPTER 38

L ittle Neck leaned on a rail fence smoking and studying the photograph Delaney had given him to see. He wore a brown blanket coat tied at the waist with a red sash, leather breeches, and high moosehide moccasins folded down to make cuffs. His name was Archibald, but his Gwich'in wife and her family called him Little Neck. He preferred it to his given name.

Smoke from a smouldering firepit drifted over the half dozen moosehide tents in the bush camp. It hung in the branches of several scrub spruce. One tent was made of thatch held down by lumbered boards. The ground around the tents was flat, and the underbrush had been cleared from between the tree trunks. Meat and fish dried on wooden racks.

Little Neck's wife joined him at the fence. He showed her the photograph. She wore a cone-shaped hood and a colourful dress shaped like a triangle. Little Neck nodded toward Delaney and said something to his wife that made the soft features of her round face plim with laughter.

"We should go," Little Neck said to Delaney, and handed him back the photograph. He pointed to the white clouds in a blue sky, a few of them hanging on mountaintops as though pinioned by the peaks.

Delaney wrapped the photograph in a canvas packet and shoved it into the inside pocket of his grey blanket coat.

Little Neck hoisted the canoe above his head and carried it from camp to the river. Delaney shouldered Little Neck's pack and another pack of camp gear. He returned up the winding path for his own pack and a canvas tarpaulin.

Little Neck's wife handed him hardtack and smoked meat, which she had wrapped in birchbark. He skidded down the riverbank and stowed the gear between the cross braces and covered it with the tarp.

They shoved off and dropped down river two miles in no time. They passed through a far-reaching stand of white pine, which quickly thinned to stunted spruce and bald mountains.

Little Neck pointed to the mountains and nodded. "Two weeks," he said. He held up as many fingers to emphasize how little time they had to get there and back.

For the next few miles the river remained ten chains wide, but started running fast. The wind seemed to squall up from behind, tearing spray off the tops of waves. Up ahead they heard the coal-chute rumble of the rapids. The river curved one way, then another. Suddenly, they were running white water.

The bow kicked out and slapped down hard, again and again. Delaney bailed as Little Neck, smiling for the challenge, danced the canoe around big boulders and through boiling eddies that threw up sheets that poured over the side.

"The whole river is jumping up and down!" Delaney shouted.

Little Neck paddled hard to keep the force of the river from catching them broadside. He skirted another boulder with a wide sweep of the paddle. Then a side-wave caught them full and flung the canoe into a whirlpool of water. Little Neck balled his back and dug deep with the paddle. He grunted with the power of each stroke to break free from the swirl of water. He dug his paddle and pulled like hell. The canoe shot clear of the boulder and through the wall of whirling water. It plunged with the river and into a chute that cut through a sharply rising scarp of rock. They hit the chute full-bore, then the water bottomed out to a hole that rammed their asses up around their shoulders.

They rounded another bend and the river widened and settled. The canoe scudded the current like a cloud. An hour later, Little Neck turned the canoe for a sandy cove. Delaney collapsed on the beach, wheezing for breath and coughing.

Little Neck made camp. Later they threw lines for trout. Little Neck caught two and Delaney one. They blackened the fish on sticks over the fire.

Little Neck heard him stir uncomfortably most of the night. In the morning, over thick, black sheep mud coffee boiled in a can and a plate of beans and hardtack soaked in fried pork fat, Little Neck said, "An old man's back doesn't ride rough water too good."

"No, it doesn't," Delaney said. "I have hurt climbing my spine and into my head."

"It won't get easier," Little Neck said. "It's a hard climb this time of year. A mudslide closed off the easy route. This one's a lot harder than you expect. Getting back could be even harder."

Delaney looked at the mountain range. "I have to make it," he said, and reached for his pack. "I have to."

Little Neck opened both hands and held them up. "Five days in, five out." He slung his pack over his shoulders and they set out.

The trail climbed sharply and followed the river for a mile or so. It then swung inland and cut through a pass in the mountains. Though it ran level for the first day's travel, the going was rough and rocky, and muddy too from heavy rains the week before. When they weren't ducking around boulders and losing their footing over loose rocks, they slogged through ankle-deep mud.

That night they camped near a deep gorge with a branch of the river plunging through it. Delaney gathered deadwood and Little Neck made a fire inside a circle of stones. They lay silently beside it. Delaney thought about Jimmy and Jane and the three children, and about the winter and summer he had spent with them, knocking rust off his carpentry skills, and working side by side with his son and grandson, and sometimes with Gabby Baker and Ted Hahn. Baker had high praise for Jimmy Delaney. His story about Jimmy saving Henry Kitchen from being crushed to death by a logging sled grew with each telling. Thomas never tired of hearing it. Neither did Delaney.

Now, as Delaney lay by the campfire, he heard the underbrush come alive with small animals. Little Neck banked the fire for the night and settled in for sleep. Delaney lay awake a while longer. He read the stars the way he and Thomas had done, stretched out in the field behind the new barn. Talking his life to his grandson.

The winter nights before the hearth, warming up to one another, talking and singing and whittling a wooden doll for young Mary, the homeyness of it, the sense of belonging. He wanted it for Robina. All of them together. A family, like he had promised Mary.

Jane had begged him to stay. Thomas had refused to see him off. Mary had pouted, but not for long.

"If you find her, you bring her here," Jimmy had said. "There's a place for her here, a home."

Hardly a home was that house on a side street in Winnipeg, Delaney remembered. A barber knew the place. He knew the names of most of the girls who worked there. Robina had been one of them.

"Gone to hell is where she went," that Prichard woman had said, her smoke-ravaged voice like a needle digging for a sliver.

"She's my daughter," he had said, and craned to see into the dark hallway. Seeing a dark-haired girl looking out at him.

Prichard had fussed at her hair and smirked. "I tell my girls they don't have fathers and they don't have mothers. They have me." She shut the door and would not open it.

Delaney and Little Neck woke before sunrise and walked as morning light played across the scarp of stone. A few times they stopped to watch the light accenting the ripple of white water around fallen, broken boulders, which had calved from the cliff. They squeezed past an outcrop of rock overhanging a waterfall. It had the shape of a serpent's head. Scratched at the base of it were several zigzag lines, circles, spirals.

"What do they mean?" Delaney asked Little Neck.

Little Neck shrugged and kept walking.

Delaney caught up and said, "We draw crosses. They mean something. In prison the soldiers carved crosses into posts."

Little Neck kept walking.

"Some of the men prayed on the crosses they drew."

Little Neck stopped for Delaney to catch his breath. Delaney sat on a boulder.

"What did they pray for?" asked Little Neck.

"Some prayed to live. Others to die. Some just prayed for more food."

"What did you pray for?"

Delaney looked at Little Neck. "Three years in hell and you change your mind about a lot of things. Even the officers stopped praying."

The third day was all uphill, skirting a glacier-carved canyon that was blood-coloured with the setting sun. They reached a plateau and made camp. They woke to pouring rain. It slowed their climb. By the time they reached the second of four switchbacks, the wind had picked up and was now blowing strong. Delaney caught a gust that stepped him back on the narrow ledge. Little Neck pointed for them to go back and wait out the blow. They returned to the bend in the first switchback where there was a shallow cave in the rock face.

There were signs in the cave that others had done the same. Empty tins of beans and meat were scattered about. Carbon stains on the rock floor marked where those others had made a fire. There was the usual graffiti on the walls. At the back of the cave there was kindling and several chunks of dried wood.

They nursed the damp kindling into a smoky fire that stung their eyes. For Delaney, memories danced among the cinders. He fixed on one the way he had in prison, dreaming himself through his loneliness by remembering the good times before death had started growing in Mary's belly. He remembered the afternoon when they had met on the footbridge across the canal.

He had blocked her way. Arms crossed and a feigned stern expression. He said, "There's a toll for passing."

"And who died and left you toll collector?" Mary had smiled, happy to play his fool's game.

"Bridge master himself," Delaney had said. He held out his hand for payment, as though demanding her to dig a coin from a pocket in her plain grey skirt. "A pittance," he said, and wiggled his fingers. "The toll is a small promise."

"Promise?"

"To stroll the path along the Fergus River. Sunday afternoon, if you like?"

He opened his eyes to the firelight playing up the walls of the cave. He pulled the canvas packet from his inside coat pocket and unfolded it to look at the photograph.

The following day it rained steady on the mountain, and once, for about an hour, it snowed. They were big flakes that melted fast but fell heavy with the promise of winter. The rain and snow stopped. Delaney and Little Neck started out in grey light. Though the sun poked out now and again, the ledge was still slippery underfoot.

They took it slow, at times walking sideways and pressing their backs to the cliff face. At other times, fallen stones forced them closer to the edge. For Delaney, each step became more difficult to take. Thoughts of Robina and Jimmy's family kept him going.

They were at the tight bend in the last of the switchbacks when Delaney's left foot slipped. His left leg slid with it and shot out into thin air.

Little Neck lurched and grabbed his pack. He dragged Delaney back on the ledge, where Delaney caught a handhold of sharp stone. He pulled his body against the cliff wall. He glanced over the side. There was nothing but sheer rock straight down.

So easy to step out into nothing, he thought. Fall like a loose stone to the barren below. So easy. No thoughts. Just nothing and no more.

He withdrew from the edge and curled into a tight ball. He smelled his sweat and the dry stink of the rock face. Between breaths, he heard a scuffing of stone, then a high-pitched bleating.

Little Neck walked forward to a bend in the ledge. He beckoned, and Delaney joined him. They saw a flock of Dall sheep gaily scampering up a nearby scarp and down another. Their fleece was pure white against the dark grey stone.

Early that afternoon, the ledge widened and opened to a tabletop with a panoramic view of the valley below. In the distance, they saw log buildings, tents, and board shacks scrambled together at the oxbow of the river.

"I'll wait here," Little Neck said. "They don't want a white Gwich'in down there."

CHAPTER 39

T he saloon was the largest building in town, and crowded with miners drinking off the profit from their diggings. The bar was a wide pine plank set across two barrels. Across from the bar, five miners played blackjack with poker faces. There was also a fair-sized dance floor where two miners danced with each other to music hammered out by an overripe woman on a thin-sounding upright piano. There was a stove on one side of the room, surrounded by round tables and ladder-back chairs, some with broken spindles. A water barrel sweated in a corner.

"You want whisky or hooch?" the bartender asked. Whisky had been packed in from the outside; hooch had been distilled in a backroom on a makeshift stove.

Delaney shook his head.

The bartender shrugged. He had seen more than enough miserable-looking men. "You got a claim? You got a food cache?"

Again Delaney shook his head. He carried and wore what he owned; grey blanket coat, grey tuque, mitts, a bedroll, and a pack stuffed with enough hardtack and smoked meat to feed two travellers back along the trail.

The bartender scowled. "A man comes in with no cache, no claim, he's a goddamn fool, mister man. Winter snow and dark is what you don't want to see. Not here. There ain't food in this camp to feed one extra mouth, you understand?"

Delaney nodded. "I'm looking for a woman. Her name is . . ."

"Don't matter," the bartender said. He looked Delaney up and down. "You need to buckle up and get out while the cliff walk is clear."

The bartender started down the bar to serve another customer.

"Her name is Robina Delaney."

The bartender stopped, turned back, shook his head sadly, and pointed to a side window that was glazed with whisky bottles. "She has the shack that stands off on its own. You'll know it."

The mining town was a hunch of earth-covered log buildings closely surrounded by board shacks and canvas tents, all belching smoke from stovepipe chimneys. Pack horses and carts had moiled the main street and side streets into one giant slough of mud.

Delaney slogged through the mud and the dark in the direction the bartender had pointed. He found the shack easy enough, the one off on its own, the one that had seen worse times and more bad weather than any of the others. It was also the one that had a man coming out and another going in.

Delaney removed his pack to a dry spot on the ground and sank onto a plank bench that had been set outside the door. He heard the goings on inside. After a while, the door opened, lamplight flashed, and a man with a bushy black beard stumbled out hitching up his braces. He grinned at Delaney and plodded off through the mud.

A dark-haired woman stood in the lit doorway. A thin shift covered her. She wore the life she had lived on her face. There were tiny scars at each side of her mouth, and a flattened cheekbone. There was a haunting distance in her eyes, and a careless, almost hopeless manner to the way she leaned on the jamb.

Delaney took all this in at once. He rose and stepped into the light from the open door. "Are you Robina Delaney?"

"Most don't care if I'm anyone," she said, her voice throaty.

"I care," he said. "I'm your father."

Robina stared at him with eyes like agates. She moaned, covered herself with her arms, and slumped sideways against the jamb. She moaned again, this time deeper, from a place inside that had been numb to feeling for a long, long time. Her face fell apart with shame.

Delaney reached, but she drew back in a start and angrily slammed the door on him. He heard her breathing behind the door. He touched the wooden planks as though trying to touch something that was touching her. He remembered Robina once hiding behind the stove to escape his tickling fingers and burning her forehead. She had come out crying and into his arms and wanting him to kiss it better.

From his inside coat pocket, he pulled the canvas packet. He removed the photograph. The image had nearly faded away. He slid it under the plank door. He returned to the bench and slung his elbows out over his knees.

"There was a song your mother sang most nights," he said softly, hoping she could hear him through the door. "Do you remember?" He hummed a bit of it.

Robina squealed angrily and hammered the door planks.

He waited for her to settle, then said, "Talk won't soften it, Robina. I doubt anything I say will make it go away."

He hunched into his coat and pulled down his tuque. His mind wandered through a wintry landscape. A ray of lamplight squeezed through a crack between the door planks and fell across the mud like a shiny gold chain that someone had dropped and forgotten. He reached out and let the chain of light fall across the burn scars on the back of his hands. Slowly he turned his hands so the light lay across the scars on his palms. He held his hands steady, as though balancing the light above the mud.

"We kept vigil over her," he said. "Jimmy couldn't stay awake, and Annie was too young. I kept saying 'Mary' over and over, and you said 'Mommy' a hundred times. You asked me, 'What will we do without her?' I was so scared. I hugged you tight, and you hugged me. It was a loss we shared, Robina. A loss that could never be filled."

Her feelings broke like a wave. She sobbed.

He stood and approached the door and listened until her scuffling fell quiet and her sobbing eased to sniffles and then to silence. He returned to the bench.

"It took me years, years."

He wiped his eyes.

"I had nothing to follow. I tried, Robina, but there were no records kept for any of you. Wherever I went I asked everyone I met, and nothing. Nothing!"

She groaned and slapped the door.

"One day I heard some railway man say Annie's name," he continued. "I found her grave in Ontario. Beside it was her child's grave."

"Oh, God," Robina cried.

"I took a rubbing off Annie's marker. There was nothing written for her child, not even a name."

From his coat pocket he took out a charcoal rubbing. He slid it under the door.

"I kept looking," he said. "I found Jimmy and his family on a prairie farm. And I found that house in Winnipeg and that miserable Prichard woman. Your friend there helped me find you from what you told her about running to the ends of the Earth."

Again she kicked the door. "Go away," she cried. "Just go away."

"I can't go away," Delaney said. He reached out his hands so the chain of light again fell across them. "I never stopped thinking of you. I never stopped loving you."

"My father's dead," she screamed, and kicked the door and pounded on it.

Delaney waited. When Robina settled, he said, "Jimmy's wife said there are no straight lines in the world. That's why it's so easy to get ourselves lost. Her and Jimmy want us to go there. They said it's a home for all of us. It's not too late, Robina. It can't be too late."

Robina fell silent.

He carefully balanced the light in the palms of his hands, as though he feared if he didn't it would break. Days of climbing exhausted him. Slowly, reluctantly, he lowered his hands and hunched into his coat. He closed his eyes and slumped into his tired body. His mind got lost amidst a swirl of random memories. Before long he fell asleep.

He woke to a grey morning. He went to the door of the shack and listened. He heard his daughter stirring inside. "Robina," he called softly. He called her name a second time.

"I don't know you," she insisted. "My father died a long time ago." She pushed the photograph and charcoal rubbing under the door to him. "I'm not going with you. This is who I am."

He pressed his head against the door and cried. On the other side of the door, she cried too.

"This is my hell," she said. "It's mine. Go away. Please go away."

"I can't go away, Robina," he sobbed. "I'm afraid to. I'm afraid I'll always be looking back, over my shoulder, looking back, and you won't be there."

After a long silence, he pushed away from the door and sat on the bench. His feet and hands twitched. He got off the bench and walked to the main street and looked across the valley to the plateau where Little Neck was camped. He looked at the grey sky and worrying clouds. He walked back and sat on the bench.

"The road has been my punishment, Robina. Punishing me for the wrong I done. All these years and . . ."

He cried and heard her crying too.

"I won't believe there is nothing left for us," he said. "There has to be."

He buried his face in his hands and sat that way for the longest time. He wrestled with the thought of time on the run. A pendulum swinging wildly. Then he heard Robina whisper, "How many miles to Babylon?"

He pulled his face out of his hands and got off the bench and went to the door and whispered, "Three score miles and ten."

He waited with his eyes closed and his hands folded. He waited. And waited.

At last she said, "Can we get there by candlelight?"

Through his tears he said, "If our heels are nimble . . ." He broke down sobbing.

Robina said, ". . . and our toes are light . . ."

He pressed both hands against the door. Shaking. "We can get there, Robina. We can get there by candlelight."

ACKNOWLEDGEMENTS

T hanks to Parks Canada, Fisheries and Oceans Canada, New Brunswick Museum, Maritime Museum of the Atlantic, the network of provincial museums throughout the Maritime Provinces, as well as the sawmills, pulp mills, logging operations, in-shore fishers, historians and archaeologists, and backcountry guides in the Yukon — all helped with my historical research over the past forty years.

Special thanks to the staff at the Public Archives of Nova Scotia for directing me to the court case of Arthur Delaney, and to the people of Atlantic Canada for their willingness to teach and share.

Mike Parker's *Woodchips & Beans* filled in much about life in the lumber woods. Frederick William Wallace's *Wooden Ships and Iron Men* did the same for shipbuilding and seafaring.

Thanks to Florence, Janet, Fred, Mary, and my clutch hitter for reading the manuscript, and to Emily Schultz for her editor's expertise.

Thanks, Jack, for taking a chance.